All I wanted to do was prove my husband hadn't embezzled and collect his retirement. I hadn't expected this…

I awoke with a crushing feeling, like my old hot flashes had come back. Suffocating heat crawled over me without the relief of cooling perspiration. Then I realized the problem was not inside me but outside.

Someone had entered the house.

We hadn't changed the locks yet, was my first thought. It was supposed to happen today. I leaped out of bed, tangled in the sheet, and fell to the floor before I could reach the bedroom door to check it. I didn't remember locking the bedroom door.

Before I could untangle my legs I felt hard hands grabbing my arms and holding them behind me as they pulled me to my feet. Fear made my legs tremble and dried out my mouth so that I couldn't scream if I had wanted to. Rough hands wrapped a blindfold around my eyes, and it didn't seem to take a minute before my hands were tied in front of me. Callused fingers moved against my neck and pressed, and everything turned black.

Edwina Hartley is a housewife in her early sixties, a recent widow after thirty-five years of marriage where she filtered all of her thoughts and ideas through her husband, George's, eyes. She now has to think for herself, and it doesn't come easy. When George died, he left behind a chaotic swamp, and Edwina is completely lost. He turned out to be a closet gambler, cashing in their insurance policies and mortgaging their palatial home. No doubt, he thought when he retired in a few months, he could recoup some of what he'd lost. Apparently, he didn't count on dying. Then the CEO of the accounting firm where George worked for twenty-five years comes to tell Edwina that they suspect George of embezzling $50,000 and, of course, they won't be honoring his retirement. And a threatening bookie begins to call, telling her that just because George is dead, it doesn't excuse his gambling debts, which she is now expected to pay. Next, the banker calls to say that George was in arrears, and she has to catch up the mortgage or they will have to foreclose. So now she not only has to prove that he never embezzled any money—or else find another source of income to make up for his lost retirement—she also beings to suspect that George didn't die of natural causes…

KUDOS for *When Angels Sleep*

"I've enjoyed all of Pinkie's books, but she hit a home run with When Angels Sleep. It engaged my interest on every page. Funny and suspenseful, Edwina is witty and wise. So fun to read." ~ Jannifrer Hoffman, author of *Secrets of the Heart*, *Random Fire*, and romantic suspense

"Some marriages are riddled with secrets, and Edwina's husband left many after his death. In this story of surviving widowhood with a sense of humor, only Edwina's tenacity—and a determined detective—can unravel the mysteries of money, the mob, and how to serve a subpoena to a tattooed biker." ~ R.L. George, author of *A Thousand Reasons*

"*When Angels Sleep* by Pinkie Paranya is the best one of the many I have read. I love the characters. They are so vivid and believable. When I did put the book down, the characters stayed with me, and I eagerly picked it up again. Well done, it's a great read." ~ Ellynore Seybold, Author *of Love's Dangerous Challenge, Sigrit,* and *Released*

"Pinkie Paranya has done it again! Her latest novel is well written and entertaining with a mix of humor and mystery. Go along on the adventure with Edwina to solve the clues to what really happened to her husband, George and all that money. A definite must-read!" ~ Debbie Lee, author of *The Journey to Jordan* and *To Love A Marine*

"I first met the character of Edwina Hartley in a short story that was included in Paranya's *Life in a Nutshell*. I said then that I wished there was a novel in the future for this character as I didn't want my time with her to end so quickly. *When Angels Sleep* fulfilled that wish beyond expectations. This starting-over-late-in-life story that takes the Chanel-clad Edwina from pampered housewife to process server to kidnap victim and more is a fast-paced heart-warming adventure filled with a cast of kooky characters and brilliant dialogue to match, as only Paranya can dish it up. Delicious!" ~ Wendy Morgan

"I'm a prolific reader of thousands of books but *When Angels Sleep* had me enthralled from the beginning to the end. Edwina's sense of humor and courage at times when she might have been scared spitless, her remarkable friendship with her side-kick Fern, her ability to begin a new life, all intrigued me. I chuckled out loud in places and held my breath in others. Paranya outdid herself." ~ Donna Garrett

ACKNOWLEDGMENTS

I want to thank all who helped edit this book and offer suggestions. Also I appreciate my loyal readers who stick with me, no matter how many genre lines I cross.

I've had a few publishers over the years, but Black Opal Books has been the best. That includes their persnickety editor Faith, who helps keep my words the best they can be, and Jack, the cover artist, who always gives me a wonderful cover.

OTHER BOOKS BY
PINKIE PARANYA
AND
BLACK OPAL BOOKS

Amazon Treasure

Death Has No Dominion

Herr Schnoodle and McBee

Love Letters in the Wind

One…Two…Buckle My Shoe

Raven Woman

Tiana ~ Gift of the Moon

Sedna ~ North Star Raven Woman

Romancing a Tasmanian Cowboy

When

Angels

Sleep

Pinkie Paranya

A Black Opal Books Publication

GENRE: COZY MYSTERY/WOMEN SLEUTHS/AMATEUR SLEUTHS

This is a work of fiction. Names, places, characters and incidents are either the product of the author's imagination or are used fictitiously, and any resemblance to any actual persons, living or dead, businesses, organizations, events or locales is entirely coincidental. All trademarks, service marks, registered trademarks, and registered service marks are the property of their respective owners and are used herein for identification purposes only. The publisher does not have any control over or assume any responsibility for author or third-party websites or their contents.

When Angels Sleep

Chapter 1

I miss George, but at the moment, I'd kill him if he wasn't already dead." I shook my head, trying to clear my thoughts. *Thirty-five years is a long time to invest in a husband and then find out he had a secret life.* Crying for days, I was running on empty. "Poor George, we needed more time together. He was just on the verge of retirement, and we'd made so many plans."

"I know, sweetie." Fern patted my back as if I'd been one of her grandchildren. "Are you sure you don't have any money left?" she asked, trying to get me off the subject. Fern had repeated that same question until I'd lost count, but then she was like that. I loved my best friend, but she was a repeater, always had been. Anything worth saying once was worth repeating at least five times. It had been the same since our college years.

It was two weeks since George passed on. My shock and grieving had evolved into numb acceptance—until today, when panic set in. I'd never been alone in my life and it frightened the heck out of me.

"George Junior was here for the funeral. Didn't you tell him any of this?"

"No, and don't you dare tell him. I don't want Junior to know about his father." No one had ever called our son Junior to his face, not even when he was a child. He was always George Two.

Fern looked shocked. "Edwina Hartley! I can't believe you said that. He's what, now? Twenty-nine going on forty? Junior's earning a ton of money. He still dabbles in stocks, doesn't he? He could help you."

"Absolutely not! I never want him to know his father should have been a charter member of Gamblers Anonymous."

"Why not? That is so dumb. First your parents spoiled you rotten and then George took over the job. And you let him," Fern accused. "You should have insisted on knowing about your finances. Then you wouldn't be in this pickle. Junior would ignore the innuendos against you."

Fern was right, even if she was prone to making up her own words. This time I didn't know what she meant by innuendos but since that wasn't part of her normal vocabulary, I let it pass. Had I asked George, he would have patted me gently on the head and ignored my questions.

He had balanced the checkbooks, helped me grocery shop, suggested our menus, and had our cars serviced at the proper time. He would have felt challenged if I'd ever asked him about finances. It was just easier to let him lead.

Even so, I suspected a little of Fern's nagging was sort of Venus envy. If George had put me up on a pedestal, her husband was the opposite. As a retired Marine, now a city fire fighter, Joe insisted everyone had to pull his own weight.

"What'll you do?"

"I've got a house full of antiques to sell."

Fern almost jumped up and down in sudden excitement. "I know, I know! In the *Antique Merchandiser* it lists all kinds of markets. We could rent a U-Haul, travel over the country, peddling antiques. Joe wouldn't mind. He'd enjoy the peace and quiet. Doesn't that sound like fun?"

I raised an eyebrow to give that look she called "supercilious" when she was showing off her crossword puzzle proficiency. "Ugh! I hate to travel. Waking up in a strange hotel room in an unfamiliar place is not my idea of a fun thing to do. By the way, have *you* ever pulled a—a trailer?"

"You're an old poop," she scolded, folding her arms over her skinny bosom.

"So, I'm not the adventurous sort." I agreed. "But maybe I'd better start looking for a job."

"Yeah. You're qualified for what?" She made imaginary tickings off her fingers, coming up with zero. "I know! You could be one of those senior Wal-Mart greeter persons."

I snorted, none too politely. Senior at sixty and three quarters? I think not. I'd never accused Fern of subtle sarcasm, but she was right. I had no talents. I met George during my third year of college. I was a late starter, living at home there was no pressure to find my niche in the world. Finally I'd decided to go to college. George Hartley was the professor of economics, a remote, handsome icon to his young, female students. I majored in art. Definitely not a good career move, I discovered later. Immediately I became attracted to George's stable, secure personality. The fact that he was twelve years older than me never mattered during our marriage. My parents had been older when they had me and tried to cushion me from any of life's hardships and indulged me unconditionally. When they died in a head on crash with a drunk driver, I fell into a deep hole. George turned out to be my life saver.

"God knows, I didn't want all this." I included the expensive antique living room furnishings in the sweep of my arm. "I'll have to give the house back to the bank."

"That's tough. I love this place. My neighborhood's getting really dumpy. Transitional, they call it."

She was exaggerating, of course. Frankly, I envied *her*. She lived in a typical blue-collar neighborhood with white picket fences, rose bushes, dogs barking in the front yards, and bikes and toys all over the sidewalks. Nice people lived on her block, not like on mine. I didn't know anyone on this cul-de-sac street. The real estate woman had called it *upward mobility* and all the young execs stayed only long enough to transfer somewhere new, dragging their families behind like tails on a kite.

"That damn chandelier in the dining room will be the first item in my yard sale," I pronounced. "When I think of how many times I'd climbed up a ladder to clean that sucker with a toothbrush before George had the remote mechanism installed."

"Yard sale!" Fern's voice squeaked up a couple of octaves until her plucked eyebrows receded into her bangs. "You wouldn't dare have a yard sale in this neighborhood."

"Who do I need to impress? Our country club dues expire this month. Word got around fast. Everyone but me, it seems, knew about George's addiction to gambling."

They hadn't ever been friends of mine but I could have sworn they liked George. I hated to admit it, but it hurt to realize their congeniality over the years was only like a thin layer of dust that had vanished already.

Fern looked smug. She always was a little resentful of our country club crowd. I caved in and told her what she needed to know. Should have done it years ago.

"They were George's buddies. I wouldn't trade a

dozen of them for one of you, girlfriend," I said.

"Gee—Eddie," she stammered and looked away.

Being friends for so many years, we never translated our feelings into words. We had met in college and our friendship was just always there.

"You know I don't like the name Eddie."

"I could call you Weenie."

"You wouldn't dare!"

She laughed. "Well, I've told you a few several times that's a dumb name. Who would name their kid Edwina?"

"And I've told you a dozen several times that it's a family name. Being an only child and my parents wanting a son so badly, they named me after my father and grandfather, Edward."

"Silly idea. It's a wonder you didn't tack that name on Junior."

I had to laugh at that idea. It hadn't occurred to me at the time.

"How are your neighbors doing? They must know George passed on."

"They cluck their tongues and try to look sad when we meet. They accepted George's gambling as an eccentricity, I suppose, but our strained financial circumstances are not tolerable. Everyone we used to know avoids me like the plague."

"Good riddance, I say. I always told you they were a bunch of phonies. You can make a killing on this place;

real estate is sky high. Why take some crummy job you're going to hate?"

"Haven't you heard a word I've said? The property is mortgaged to the roof. George owed a lot of people. Judging from the phone calls I've received since he's been gone, I hope I never meet some of them."

"Someone's threatened you? George's bookies? My lord, you've unplugged a hornet's nest."

I wondered how much I dared tell her. She might get Joe involved, and her husband had a temper fuse about the size of a birthday candle. You couldn't throw tantrums at the kind of people George had been dealing with.

"No, of course no one's threatened me, you're watching too much TV again," I lied. Ever since George's passing, a gravely-voiced man had called, wanting to know how his bets were going to be paid off.

"Can bookies collect on a dead person's gambling debts?" Fern's question told me she was as ignorant as I had been about that subject, but the man on the phone set me straight in a heck of a hurry.

"Apparently, they don't forgive gambling debts just because someone has the audacity to die." That sounded cold, but George had left me in such a mess that I was becoming very annoyed with him since his hasty departure, and I was beginning to think he got the better deal. I swiped at tears that traitorously crept from under my closed eyes. I did miss him so. We might not have had what a romance novel would call a tempestuous love affair, but we had a solid, caring, nurturing, and sometimes great enthusiasm that surprised both of us. Of course eagle eye Fern noticed the stray tears.

"Aw, Eddie, I know how much you two loved each other. But you have to go on." She hugged me, and I wanted to bawl, but gritted my teeth and thanked her.

George's double life had destroyed my sense of well-being, leaving me feeling as secure as a Chihuahua in a yard full of pit bulls. How could he fool me like that? How could I be so trusting? Worse, how could he not confide in me, ask me for help or at least comfort? Was I such a completely useless person? I recall several times wandering into his study, when he worked late at the computer, and asking him what he was doing. He gave me the same cryptic answer.

"When angels sleep, men bring on the demons."

I often wondered what he meant and always thought I'd ask him. Now it was too late.

I could close my eyes and hear him say that and then wave his hand to tell me to close the door behind me. Now, when I took time to think about it, that was very uncharacteristic of him, since he was always so steadfastly pleasant to be around.

"Okay, strip the house, sell the furnishings, let the bank take the property, and then what? *Then* will you tell Junior?"

"He idolized his dad. You know how close they

were." A wave of sadness washed over me when I thought of the contradiction in using a word like "close" to describe either George or Junior. I felt a nervous giggle erupt.

"What's so damn funny?"

"I'm just jumpy. Everything's moving so fast, I feel like my nerves are perched on the edge of my skin, waiting to fall out."

"It's got to be hell, sweetie. You're the laid-back, calm one. Hang in there. You can get through it. I always say once a bad thing starts, it's like a snowball rolling down hill, building up steam. But at the bottom, it will all float away."

She could make me smile through anything. "The problem is, I can't sell any of it until after probate. It still galls me to know that George made his lawyer executor of the estate. Couldn't even trust me to do that right. Junior is upset. He thought he should be the one. But I see why George did it. He didn't want Junior to know about the canceled insurance policies and the debts."

"Won't Junior find out when the lawyer reads the will?"

"Don't think so. No reason for any of that to come out." *Yet.*

"I bet Junior is going to want some of this old stuff. George told Joe and me how much he paid for that Hepplewhite sideboard in the dining room. All the furniture in our house didn't cost as much."

"Tell me about it. And now the very people he tried so hard to impress are looking right through me as if I'm invisible. Do wives turn invisible after their husbands die?"

She shrugged. "Depends. I've heard it happens. Whoever does that to you is no great loss. You're a much finer person than any of them."

"Ah, you're a dear, Fern. Don't know what I'd do without you."

We subsided into a vacuum of embarrassed silence. With Fern I knew it wouldn't last long.

"When do you start working on your problem then?" she asked.

I looked at her, not getting the connection with the rest of our discussion. Fern is like that. Totally from the sky, she can pull out a topic we'd been discussing the day before, a week before, and take off with it.

But it only stumped me for a second. I was proud of my ability to catch her loose ends. "Looking for a job? I don't know. Soon. If I can forestall the bank from fore-closing until I find a place to live, if I can keep the book-ies from fitting me with cement overshoes…Problem is, everything needs to be done yesterday. I'm working against time."

That conversation over, she went home to watch her talk shows, and I sat down to try and figure out what to do with the rest of my life.

Chapter 2

When I opened my door the next afternoon to the impatient sound of chimes, the two men in suits made my heart almost stop. My first thoughts centered with the strange voices on the phone about George's gambling debts. I could feel my size eights encased in cement shoes. Did they still do that? I didn't want to know.

"Mrs. Edwina G. Hartley?" The older man stepped forward, but discreetly not past the threshold. "My name is Jordan, Alexander Jordan, and this is John Carroll. We're from Graham, Graham, and Wilbur. Please forgive the intrusion in your time of mourning."

A big sigh escaped before I could shut it off. They were from the accounting firm where my husband had worked. They probably wanted to talk to me about his pension. I could use some good news. Odd that they wouldn't call me into the office.

"Come in. I'll get some coffee," I offered, motioning them into the living room.

They declined with duplicate shakes of their heads and, once inside, they sat on the edge of the rosewood brocaded sofa and looked around as if totaling my assets. I began to get a very uncomfortable feeling. I waited and finally Mr. Jordan spoke.

"We…we uh…we are sorry about your loss."

Somehow I didn't think that was why they came to call.

"Are you here about George's retirement?" I'd always been a direct sort of person.

The younger man actually flinched and looked down at his shoes. Not a good sign.

Jordan cleared his throat. "Actually—we have some bad news."

My husband was dead. He had canceled his life insurance policies. His bookies threatened me almost daily. I couldn't pay the mortgage on the house. So, their bringing bad news came as a definite anticlimax.

"There is a problem concerning your husband's retirement. You see, when he died so precipitously, we checked into his accounts."

"And?" I prompted impatiently. I never liked bandages pulled off slowly, a little at a time.

"I'm afraid, pending further investigation, we will

have to hold his retirement. You see…ah…there are some discrepancies in his accounts. Actually, embezzlement is strongly indicated."

"What?" I leaped from the chair, knocking the flimsy thing backward to the floor.

They held their briefcases in front of them as shields, pulling up their knees. Their clone-like behavior stopped my outrage for just a second and I wanted to giggle. I did that when I was close to hysteria.

"What are you trying to pull here? George wouldn't embezzle a dime. He worked at your corporation for over twenty years and counted on that retirement—it was due him. This was his last year before retirement."

"I know this is unexpected. We didn't want to tell you over the phone, but perhaps…" The younger man looked fidgety, as if he'd rather be anywhere else.

I tried to concentrate, but my thoughts bonged against the sides of my head like marbles in a jar. For a second I wondered if these men might hear the rattle.

"I'll hire an attorney and contest this. It isn't right. You're trying to save the company money by denying George's retirement besides calling him a thief." I stared at them in my best chairman of the board manner. I had held that position in PTA for years while Junior was in school and had perfected *the look* as Fern called it.

Jordan walked over to the window and touched the heavy drapes. "This is a charming home. I compliment you on your lovely antiques. My wife—"

"The house is going back to the bank, along with the furniture," I interrupted.

I didn't want to hear about his wife. I wanted to hate him. I hoped my statement about the furniture was creative fabrication. George had paid for the furniture on his credit cards. Surely he'd paid the cards off by now.

At that moment, I came near to hating George for the feeling of helplessness, of pure vulnerability sweeping over me. I'd never even asked where he kept the key to the bank safety deposit box.

"Yes, well, we can check on that later, of course," Jordan said.

"How much are you accusing George of stealing?"

"Actually *stealing* is a fairly harsh term, but in rounded figures, close to fifty thousand dollars. When a member of our firm departs, for any reason, we conduct an audit."

"Company policy," the younger man added.

"Are you saying *you* did an audit? Isn't that a bit irregular? Wouldn't your corporation hire an outside firm to investigate for you?"

Hah! A look of surprise slipped across Jordan's face before he closed it off again. Even I had to learn a little something from George's twenty years of accounting. He took his sweet time to answer, as if disdaining my question.

"No, this is an inside matter, strictly a shortage within the company. We…ah…we were hoping to be discrete in our handling it so as not to cause embarrassment to George's…ah…your family."

Too late for that. I folded my arms tight across my chest, hoping they wouldn't notice the tremor that started from my toenails and progressed up my body to the roots of my hair. "I don't believe my husband stole a dime. In the many years he worked there, he never brought home as much as a paper clip."

"We—we uh—understand he gambled on sports events, fights, horses. Some employees heard him making bets over the phone."

Sneaky bastards, was nothing sacred? Just minutes before I'd begun to hate George, now I wanted to defend him.

They headed toward the door, wisely choosing not to shake hands with me. "We'll be in touch with you soon," Jordan said stiffly, as if he'd like to say something kind, but couldn't quite manage.

When the door closed behind them, I sat at the Duncan Phyfe dining room table, put my head on the smooth dark mahogany surface, and let the tears come. When I finished crying, I wiped my eyes with a tissue, and then I got angry.

"George didn't steal any money!" I said the words out loud. He had a lot of faults, I was finding out about them in buckets full. But he'd never embezzle from his company, knowing it would jeopardize his retirement. He'd looked forward to that time in his life when he could putter around the garden and search out more antiques. We talked about an ocean cruise even. We'd never done any of that since we married.

What was I going to do? I wanted to call Fern, tell her about the latest developments, to soak up her loyal support. No use, she wasn't home. It was Friday. She'd be at the Olive Garden, having lunch with her Red Hats.

My next thought was to give up. I began to envy George his peace. This was all too much. Nothing in my life had prepared me to take care of myself, much less cope with everything that happened in such a short time.

What about George Junior? Our son worshiped his father. They were peas in a pod. If the embezzlement charge proved true—and in the light of all the other things George had neglected to tell me, it could be genuine—I had to keep the truth from him. It would destroy him. He'd built his life on his father's principles and even had planned the same career in accounting since high school. That meant I couldn't give up. Not yet. George wouldn't have embezzled from his company. I had to hold onto that. It was up to me to find a way to clear his name, and I didn't have a lot of time to do it.

I swam in shark-infested waters and looked back over my shoulder with every stroke.

Chapter 3

The morning of George's funeral, the sun refused to shine. The skies darkened with a coming storm. George Junior was scheduled to arrive at the airport early and insisted on taking a taxi instead of my meeting him. It was just as well, the idea of driving inside the airport scared the bejeebers out of me. When the doorbell rang, I ran to open the door and enfold our son in my arms as tight as our disparity in height would allow me.

He kissed the top of my head like he always did and shed his coat on the way, hanging it up precisely on the coat hanger by the door.

"Mother, you must be exhausted." He looked at me, his eyes searching my face.

Oh, lordy, he was so much like his father in every

way. Tall, erect posture with not an ounce of flab, and so handsome, with just a faint touch of gray at his temples. It sent a smothering sadness forcing me to take a deep breath. I had to be strong and not let my natural instincts of wanting to confide in someone overwhelm me. He couldn't know about George's excesses—not right now, maybe later, after he'd gone home and had time to recover from his grief.

George Junior drove us to the funeral home where we met Fern. She hugged me and then my son, tears streaming from her eyes.

"I'm so glad you could make it, Jun—ah—George Two."

I could tell by her hesitation that she was wondering if he was George One now, and the idea made my appalling need to giggle rise to the surface.

"So am I," George said, turning his head to look at her. "I'm thankful Mother has you to lean on. Is your husband here?"

Fern shook her head. "Joe felt really bad about that, but there was a four alarm fire in the business district, and he couldn't get away."

We sat through the memorial. George had always spoken of closed caskets, and I knew that was what he would have wanted. He always said he didn't want anyone looking at him when he couldn't look back. The thought sent a creeping sense of loss, but I held back my tears.

I recognized a few of the country club members who came up to speak with me. The bank manager and his wife attended but managed to stay a distance away, which wasn't a good sign. I didn't recognize anyone from his work, although we hadn't attended many company events. It was a relief not to see the two corporate honchos who had visited me.

At the gravesite, Junior and I laid roses on top of the mound of earth and quietly said our goodbyes. It had just begun to drizzle rain, and we escaped back into our car. Fern followed in hers and met us at the house. I hadn't wanted to invite anyone but Fern back with us, the phonies from the country club were the last people I wanted to see right now.

At the house, we three sat drinking coffee and eating slices of chocolate cake I'd baked last night. I thought chocolate would help cheer us, but it didn't seem to have any effect. We sat around not talking until Junior spoke into the silence.

"Mother, you must come and stay with me until this is all over. Dad's attorney can send us copies of the will and you can close up this house for now." He looked around as if saying goodbye. He was like his father, in that he'd always enjoyed living here amongst the antiques and brocades.

I thought of his austere condo in the noisy city and shuddered. Was there nowhere I wasn't out of place?

I put my hand on his arm and squeezed. "Thank you,

son, but there are matters to straighten out here that need my immediate attention."

Fern sniffed loudly, and I knew she waited for me to tell Junior some of what had happened with his father but I couldn't. Not yet. I glared at her and shook my head.

"I'm certain the insurance will pay off eventually, but do you have enough cash to carry you until then?" he asked. "I'll sign over my share of our mutual account as soon as I get back," he offered.

I didn't want him to know even part of the circumstances of his father canceling the life insurance policy and not knowing how I was to manage in the near future. My damn pride got the best of me just then and later I would kick myself for it. "That won't be necessary, really. If I ever need you to do that, I'll let you know."

When we set up the bank account, I'd foolishly insisted on *and* not *or*. Now the bank account needed both our names to withdraw. But then, how could I know I'd ever need that money? Later, I would ask for it, when I had the death certificate. But I had a sinking sensation that he might even owe IRS.

My loyalty kicked in just then, and I crossed that off. He made his tax payments way ahead of time every years since we'd been married.

Junior had to leave the next afternoon. He'd used all his vacation time and sick leave to attend a CPA conference in Boston earlier. Apparently, his company made no allowances for emergency leaves. I didn't want to see him off at a busy airport, so we said our goodbyes in the house before he left.

"Mother, if you ever need anything, please let me know. If I didn't think you would be well off with our home and the life insurance to come, I'd insist, very strongly, that you come stay with me." He bent and kissed my cheek, smoothing back the lock of hair that I had let fall forward to hide my tears.

"I will call you, my dear. But of course you'll let me know the moment you get home, won't you? I'll worry otherwise." Planes crashed—not often, but they did.

"I'll call, as usual, once a week on Sunday. I love you."

My heart almost came to a standstill. My son hadn't said those words to me since he had become a teenager. "I love you too, son. Your father loved you, you know that."

He nodded, unable to speak. Turning to leave, he gave one wave and then got into the taxi.

I was glad Fern wasn't there to see the tears and sorrow that overcame me when I closed the door. I'd never felt so alone in my life.

Chapter 4

It was hard for me to sit in the living room where George died. Every time I looked at that recliner—the pale blue satin upholstery he'd ordered because he loved that color and the feel of satin—I saw him sitting there, pale and lifeless. I made myself think of those few hours, for the first time since it happened, willing myself a catharsis. One final total recall to get it out of my head.

The television had been on as usual. George sat kicked back, as if taking a snooze. He had developed a heart murmur, and his pacemaker took care of the extra beats. He also had type II diabetes, but he could take pills to keep it under control. His energy level, never tremendous, had declined, and I worried. But he never wanted me go with him to visit his doctor.

As my memory reviewed that scene, something jarred, my stomach balled up tight. I'd come home from a program at the library. It wasn't late, maybe nine-thirty. The porch light wasn't on, which was odd, and the door was unlocked. He always made sure the porch light stayed lit when I went out at night, and he could have forgotten that, but he would never have left the door unlocked. Why did I just now remember that one of the couch pillows lay out of place on the floor near his chair? George never even laid his newspaper on the floor. That's what coffee tables were for. A chill warred with a sudden hot flash, a sure sign of distress. I rushed over to the chair and knelt to look closer at the material.

Just at the edge, where his shoulder might have rested, I saw a tiny, ugly stain. It looked like rust. I peered closer and pulled back from scratching at it just in time. I sat down on the floor and stared at the chair, hoping I was seeing spots. I blinked my eyes, but it was still there.

It wasn't rust, it was blood. My stomach clenched, and my throat dried so I had trouble swallowing. Poor George, to be all alone when this might have happened.

Could one of those bookies have slipped in that night when I was out and killed him? Could they use an ice pick, a needle, or some other terrible weapon so there wasn't a lot of blood? When I found George, I'd called 911 and our family doctor. The ambulance arrived almost at the same time. There never had been a question of foul play. Our doctor pronounced it a heart attack and the medical examiner at the hospital agreed. He said something about the pacemaker hadn't protected the top part of his heart.

Right now, poor George was lying in his grave, peaceful as could be. Still keeping secrets.

If there was blood on the chair, then his pajama top would have had a blood stain too. The mortuary gave me a plastic bag with the clothes he wore that night. I had put the bag and all in the hamper in the laundry room, until I could deal with doing away with his belongings.

In the laundry room, I fished the bag out of the hamper and strewed the contents on the folding table. I picked up George's watch, the last thing he took off at night, and held it to my cheek, hearing the gentle ticking, feeling George's essence a brief moment before it faded away. I set the watch down and reached across the blue pajama bottoms to pick up his matching pajama top, spreading it out carefully.

There, on the top edge of the material where his shoulder would have been I saw a tiny prick of dark stain. Why had no one noticed? Since there had been no hint of foul play, they probably thought of it as a normal scratch mark, if anyone even saw it. But there was that unlocked door. Had George opened it to someone? Someone he knew? I shuddered at the sudden idea of anyone having a key.

I needed to call Fern. Two heads had to be better than the head I was thinking with now. I hadn't told her about the embezzlement charges. As far as my notion of a possible murder—that was so far out I had trouble believing I'd entertained the idea for a moment. When I punched her number on my cell phone, she answered right away.

"Can you come over?" I asked. "I need to talk."

"You bet. I'll be right there."

"Are you sure you're not busy?"

"No, Joe is out of town, a fireman's convention. I feel bluesy, lower than a caterpillar's pecker. Be glad to talk to you."

When she arrived, we sat in the kitchen, my favorite room in the house. George hadn't felt the need to perfect this room as he had the rest of the house, and I'd had it painted pristine white with yellow trim and a nice picture window looking out over my herb garden at the side of the house.

I started easy-like, telling her about the embezzling charges.

"Do you believe it? That George stole the money?"

She made a good try at keeping her voice neutral, but I heard the doubts ripple beneath her words. Who wouldn't doubt George by now? I took no offense.

"For God's sake, Fern. You know he was counting the months until he retired and could putter around in our garden and buy more antiques. He might have had a lot of secrets, but he'd never jeopardize his retirement."

"That's true enough, dear. But face it. He *did* borrow

on the insurance policies without you knowing. Might have even cashed them in—"

"He paid for them," I interrupted haughtily.

"Aw, come on. Don't pull your PTA board *shtick* on me, darlin'. The point is, the insurance is gone."

"You're right," I agreed, properly chastised.

"Gambling is kinda like shooting up. When it takes hold of you, you'd do anything to keep the habit."

Those damned talk shows. She devoured them like I did romance novels. The difference was, my reading materials didn't get me involved in rape, incest, cross dressing, and lord only knows what forms of perversions the human mind was capable of inventing and displaying on daytime talk shows.

"I don't believe he stole from the firm," I insisted. "Even if he did hide his gambling from me."

"And left you destitute. Don't forget that. If only you'd had a bit of extra-century perception, you might have avoided some of this."

I knew what she meant this time. Extra sensory. "That's a little exaggerated, but yes, you may be right." I forced myself to stay calm.

For all Fern's smart mouth, she was extremely thin-skinned. She could dish it out, but she could never take it. I couldn't afford to cause friction between us now. I needed her friendship.

"How will you prove or disprove the charges of embezzlement? Have you thought of that? Even if you knew what to look for, they're not going to let you inside that office to check the books."

She knew my penchant to avoid anything mathematical. I didn't even like to use the calculator. "I might hire a private investigator," I said.

Fern giggled nervously. The giggle pricked the balloon of what I considered extreme logic.

"What's so funny?"

"That just slipped out, but what do you think you're going to pay this PI with?"

"I might just go out and get a job."

When she quit laughing, I changed the subject. "Remember when Junior was fourteen and George let him work a week on a school project? The little genius put a terrific portfolio together for me."

"Oh yeah, I remember. The account George gave you to keep your coupon money in. Wow, I hope it's federally insured."

"Don't be such a smartass. There's quite a little pile of money in the bank. I hardly touched it over the years." Early in our marriage, when I saw George was going to hang on to the purse strings, I persuaded him to let me have my own little savings account to keep for birthdays and special events I didn't want to 'bother' him about. I'd had fun with it over the years, and it had grown with Junior's help.

"Then you don't need to worry about losing your furniture and a house around your ears?"

Always the optimist. "It may not be in the million-aire class, but it would hire a detective," I said with a lot more assurance than I felt.

"When are you going?" Fern asked, cocking her head at an angle like an inquisitive bird looking for a special worm.

"Going?" I'd lost track momentarily, but figured she meant looking for a job or hiring a detective.

"You need me to go with you," she said. "Can you wait until I get back from Ernie's?" She'd promised to babysit a grandkid two states away. I was frightened to think about starting to dig around on my own, but re-lieved to think that I could. Fern's smart mouth might slow progress or complicate matters.

"I just want to check out a few investigators in the area and see what they have to offer." For the first time in my life, I wanted to do things for myself. One of my qualities was stubbornness. George had been fond of tell-ing me this often over the years, always couched in very loving terms, of course.

"There's another problem." It was time to level with her. I had to tell someone.

She looked at me, waiting.

"Something odd happened the night George died. It's very confusing, not to mention disturbing."

"Like what?"

"Someone might have—I think George might have been murdered."

Fern's eyes bugged, her mouth dropped open, and I waited for the derision. It didn't come.

"Oh, honey." She ran to hug me. "You're under such a strain. You need to get help."

"No! I'm serious. Listen to me a minute." I explained to her, for the first time since it happened, about the evening when I found George. I told her about the pillow out of place on the floor and the spot of blood.

"Did you wash it off?"

It was probably a question a private investigator—or the police might have asked. "No. Of course not. Want to see?" Without waiting for an answer, I led her into the living room and pointed at the offending chair.

Fern wore her reading glasses around her neck in an annoying necklace made with fake little pearls. I thought it was what elderly women might wear and neither of us should have been ready for that. But unlike me, she wasn't too vain to admit she needed help reading.

Perching the glasses on the tip of her nose, she bent to peer close into the fabric.

"Don't touch it!" I yelled.

Any effect of a withering glare was greatly diminished by her black and white zebra frames. When she shook her head, I read the truth in her expression, and my heart did a flip flop. Fern had worked as a registered nurse the first years of their married life. She knew blood when she saw it.

"You're sure this stain wasn't there before?"

"Uh, uh. George would have noticed and told me about it. He'd have had a crew in to clean the entire chair."

"Yeah, for sure." She looked in the direction of the big overstuffed pillow on the couch and hightailed it back into the kitchen as if the room gave her the willies. It was beginning to have that effect on me, too.

"There's more," I said.

"I expected so."

This was not easy for me. George would have loathed being murdered, as something so…so uncouth, so untidy.

Chapter 5

The pajama top he wore that night? The funeral parlor sent the clothes back, and I checked it. The stain was there, where his shoulder would have been."

"And no one noticed?"

"There wasn't any reason to suspect he died from anything but a heart attack. The lighting here is kind of dim, George preferred it that way, except for his reading lamp. His pajamas are nearly the same color as the chair. He loved that shade of blue. His doctor and I followed the ambulance to the hospital where the hospital doctor agreed and pronounced him dead officially. I saw him alone one last time."

"George's doctor didn't question anything?"

"Why would he? He's treated George for his heart

and diabetes all these years. Apparently, the hospital doctor on call didn't find anything unusual either."

"I don't know what to think."

"*You* don't. What about me? I can't decide what to do next."

"Was there a tear or hole in George's shirt? Like someone might have used a knife or...or ice pick on him?" Fern shuddered. "That's beyond creepy."

I swallowed past a dry throat. What a horrible thought. "Not that I could see. His pajama top is silk, with a kind of delicate open weave. It was just one tiny dark spot."

"What about a needle! Someone might have slipped in here and shot George up with drugs."

As weird as that sounded bubbling out of Fern, there could be some truth in it. The thought had occurred to me too. "An autopsy would have discovered drugs or poison." I finally made myself say the dreaded word, autopsy. My mind wouldn't wrap around the idea of exhuming George and a stranger cutting away on his defenseless body, so I blanked out on that picture, thankfully. "I can't go to the police, not yet."

"But who would kill George? And why?" she asked.

This was what made telling anyone else hard to do. Indeed, who and why. "One of his bookies, maybe?"

Fern snorted indelicately. "I don't think so. If they went around doing that to all their clients, how would they ever get paid?"

That made sense. "I don't know where to go with this, honestly. This may sound off the wall, but if George was murdered, and I start poking around and turn something up, what if I become a suspect?"

"Of killing George? Why? You lost your income when he died."

"But I didn't know that at the time. I assumed he had made insurance payments. Maybe they'd have some way of proving that I didn't know he'd canceled the policies. I'd have to admit it on the witness stand if they asked me."

"Do you have an alibi?"

Was she getting these ideas from *Murder She Wrote,* her favorite late night re-run?

"Not a very good one," I said. "I went to a library program. No sign-in sheets or anything like that. I don't remember seeing anyone I know."

"What kind of program?"

"Homeopathic remedies in the 2000s, I think it was called."

"Lordy, lordy, thank you for not asking me to go with you."

I managed a smile. Fern always knew how to cheer me up.

Her forehead puckered, and I let the conversation drop for a moment, tired to the bone. I'd never had to do so much serious thinking since…I didn't remember since when.

"Junior flew out to the funeral. I'm sure he would come back to help you."

Junior was a good son, but we were never close. I didn't feel guilty about that. He was born a solitary person, an adult captured in a child's body. The Chinese called it an old soul. George probably had something to do with it too, always talking such serious stuff, wanting his son to be a miniature clone of himself.

"He'd come to help me. But I don't want him to. Not until I get these questions answered. The bookies, the embezzlement charge, and now this needle business—"

"I'd wait, see if anyone contacts you," Fern advised. "You can tell the police any time later that you just noticed the spot of blood and then leave it up to them. They might order an autopsy."

"You mean exhume George?" The same thoughts I'd had, but it sounded so bizarre said out loud. That would be the final indignity to poor George.

"Say he *was* murdered. What if whoever did this wants to bump you off too? Especially if you start poking around, asking questions."

Ms. Optimist, that was Fern. "What can I do? I can't just let it go."

"Well, maybe your idea about contacting a PI isn't such a weird idea after all. He could advise you how to approach the authorities. Although at this point, maybe you'd better consider a lawyer first."

"Thanks. I'll settle for the PI if I can find one."

Poor George, you were a quiet, conservative soul in life but in death you are turning out to be singularly difficult.

The next day, I picked two names out of the phone book and started my quest.

I hesitated and almost turned away outside the shabby building of my first choice. *J. Dugan, Private Investigator, Licensed and Bonded* the lettering read. Naturally, I started with the top of the alphabet, skipping over Ace and Acme as too blatant and common. The building looked to be the most upscale on the block, which wasn't saying a whole lot for it.

I clutched my purse close and wished I'd brought along that container of mace. It wasn't much help tucked in the glove compartment of a car that might not be there when I was ready to leave this neighborhood. Over the years, George and I had an on-going argument. He wanted to buy me one of those stun-guns for my protection. As if I'd ever gone anywhere without him or as if anyone was looking to jump this slightly overweight frame of mine.

It wasn't until I twisted the door knob that I saw the sign. Closed Tuesdays.

Somewhere in the depths of my handbag hid that scrap of paper with the second name and address on the list. Large red block lettering in the next office window caught my eye.

HELP WANTED.

Curious, I walked closer. Someone had taped a clip from the newspaper to the grimy window. The temporary agency requested applicants for the position of process server. *No experience necessary, no special education required, must be reliable.* What could be more perfect for me?

Tarnished gold lettering across the top of the window spelled out *Subpoenas, Inc.* and beneath it in smaller print, *Harold Levine, Prop.* I tried that door handle.

The door opened to an office the size of my linen closet. I only wished it had been as clean.

"Hello. My name is Edwina Hartley. The temp agency sent me." I fabricated that at the last minute, remembering the newspaper clip in the window.

The man glaring at me from beneath the biggest, bushiest eyebrows I'd ever seen had to be Mr. Levine. I would have liked to be wrong, for once.

"So?"

"I'm here about your ad in the window," I persisted.

"The agency isn't getting paid to find me a freaking housewife. I need someone with balls to get the job done."

My first thought was to turn tail and run. No one had ever glared at me in that manner and certainly no one had ever spoken to me so rudely. I counted to ten and decided to give it my best effort *then* turn tail and run. What could be so difficult about being a process server? Didn't they deliver summons, divorce papers, stuff like that? I'd seen that done on TV, and surely Fern knew all about it.

"The agency sent me. They must know what you want," I insisted.

"Them bimbos don't know spit. How the hell anyone in that place holds a job is beyond me." He ruffled some papers on his desk. "What makes you think you can be a process server, just like that?" He clicked his bony fingers together and the sound was so dry, it barely made a whisper.

It seemed to undermine his confidence a bit when I didn't shout back at him or grab for a hanky. Levine could have been anywhere from forty to sixty. It was hard to guess his age with that perpetual scowl etched on his face. His head was bald in back with a little fringe of gray hair around the top. His gray-black eyebrows crashed together like mini locomotives when he frowned. This happened often.

I glanced down at the grimy chair with a crumpled pizza carton on the seat and continued to stand. "I know what process servers do." God knows, I'd be getting visits from them soon enough, from George's employers and the bank. "You give me a legal paper with the address of the recipient, and I deliver said summons or warrant or subpoena, whatever. Isn't that about it?"

He leaned his face into his palms and sighed. I think I heard a faint "*oy vey*," but couldn't be sure. I waited.

It didn't take him long to realize I was still there.

"Lady—"

"Edwina, Edwina Hartley," I prompted, hoping he would get the hint that I wasn't going away.

He cleared his throat and tried again. "Whatever. It isn't that simple. You look like a nice, sweet lady. Somebody's grandma, maybe. I gotta tell you, things get kinda hairy when you force something on a person that he don't want."

Somebody's grandma? I prided myself on taking excellent care of myself, at certain times, George even called me gorgeous. I wore my hair in a page boy that just touched the top of my shoulders, which I knew was outdated, but it suited me. By now, I didn't really know the color of my hair. I kept it ash blonde, courtesy of a well-known hair product. Fern generously referred to my one or two wrinkles as laugh lines. For heaven's sake, Reba McIntyre, the famous country singer, shared the same birthday with me.

"What could it hurt to give me a chance? You don't appear to be overrun with applicants for the job."

"No. Well, I don't carry insurance, you know— workman's comp, liability, that kind of crap. You gotta carry your own, and believe you me, sooner or later you're gonna need it."

His inventory of insurance policies wasn't reassuring. I decided he was trying to scare me and politely refrained from commenting.

"You get paid on delivery. An extra bonus comes with each third delivery. Your time's your own, pick your hours. Each packet comes with a date. You have to deliver by that date. I got a reputation to uphold."

His voice came out of his thin lips like little bullets shooting words into the air. Listening to him left me feeling out of breath.

"Sounds fair." For a welcoming speech, it could have gone better, but it looked as though I might have the job. I would use the money to hire the private investigator.

"That what you always wear?" He nodded toward my Chanel suit. It was years old and the plainest outfit in my closet. I hadn't wanted to appear affluent if I spoke to a private investigator.

"What do you suggest? Jeans and a tee shirt?" I thought I was being funny.

"That's what most of 'em wear. 'Course you do put on kind of a classy old broad front that most citizens wouldn't normally hide from. That could be a definite plus, almost like a disguise."

I cringed at his description of me, but couldn't afford to take offense. Who was he kidding? He could have been in his sixties too. He tossed his insults out so casually, he didn't even know he was being rude and wouldn't have cared if he'd known.

He pushed a manila file over the desk toward me. "I'll start you off easy. Mr. C. C. Patterson works for the county hospital as an orderly. His wife wants a divorce, but Patterson doesn't. Open and shut. Get on it. Write down your TAT before you bring back the signed affidavits." He ruffled some papers on his desk, signifying that the interview had ended.

"TAT?" I had to ask.

He cringed. "Turn-around time. How long it takes you."

"Thank you, Mr. Levine. You won't regret hiring me." I wanted to stop gushing and couldn't. I sounded disgustingly fawning to my own ears, but since it was the first job I'd ever had in my life, the sense of accomplishment felt exhilarating. Like when I learned to drive, over George's dire predictions and pleas not to do it.

That turned out fine. So, I was sure, would this. I couldn't wait to tell Fern.

Chapter 6

My clothes are too nice, Fern."

We sat on the edge of my bed, staring into the closets.

"First time I heard anyone complain about that." She fingered the lapels of the Chanel jacket I had just tossed on a chair. "When do you start work? I wish you'd consider something else. It seems kind of—"

"I know, sleazy."

"Well, maybe not that extreme, but you've never even known a soul who had to accept a warrant or a summons, have you?"

"Are you going negative on me all of a sudden?"

She grinned. "Nope. Just observating."

Fern made up her own vocabulary sometimes.

"I'll start Monday morning. He said my time's my

own, just so I get the job done by deadline." I told her about Mr. Patterson.

"That doesn't seem so hard. You just knock on his door and introduce yourself."

"Not that easy, apparently. As I see it, they can hide from a warrant or a subpoena for a long time. You have to hand it to them personally, and they have to accept it."

"Oh." Fern subsided into silence, which was unlike her. I supposed she was mulling over my dilemma.

"I'll go with you the first time." She brightened, imagining a great adventure, no doubt. Fern was not always grounded in reality, in spite of her addictions to the *Inquirer*, the *Stars* and every daytime talk show she could watch. Or maybe because of that.

"Thanks, but no. Mr. Levine might not approve of my taking a guest along on my first job." An understatement if I ever heard one.

Fern eventually went home and left me to study a plan of attack.

The telephone rang and I let it go on and on, waiting for the answering machine to kick in. No one had called me lately, without giving me some sort of bad news.

"Mrs. Hartley. Are you there?"

Oh, oh, that voice again. It reminded me of the sound of footsteps creeping along on a gravel walkway.

The voice stopped abruptly when the phone clicked off. This probably meant he didn't want to be traced. I had caller ID, but when I looked, it said "out of area."

George's bookie couldn't squeeze blood out of a turnip, could he? The metaphor made me decidedly uncomfortable.

Perhaps I should call the man, get it over with, and tell him all the bad stuff that's happened to me. Maybe he had a mother or a sister. The first time I answered the phone and he spoke on the other end of the line, I had no choice but to talk to him. His threat was real. He wanted money. Throwing myself on his mercy hadn't helped then, but now with the embezzlement thing, I had more fuel to fight with. I could see with an answering machine. He was playing it cagey. Not even a veiled threat.

One thing at a time. I needed to concentrate on my first mission—the handing over a summons to Mr. C.C. Patterson.

Piece of cake.

℮ℜℇℜ

In the hospital, I recognized several of the volunteers at the front desk. We'd known Gloria and Alice and their husbands from our country club. I asked about Mr. Patterson, and they called personnel to find out he worked on the fourth floor, afternoon shift. That meant he'd work from three p.m. to eleven p.m. I had a brilliant idea and couldn't wait to get on with it, but Gloria wanted to talk.

"I'm sorry I missed George's funeral," she said.

"Yes, well, I'm sorry too." I waited for an explanation of why she missed the funeral, but none came.

"We haven't seen you at the dinners. Are you going to start coming again?" Tall and thin, Alice wore beige over blouse and pants which made her resemble a noodle cinched in the middle with a concho belt, in spite of the regulation Pepto Bismol colored jacket.

"I don't think so." Damned if I would give her the satisfaction of telling her I planned to move from the neighborhood soon.

"Well..." Her voice drifted off, and she looked away like I was the scene of an accident.

"Guess we'd better get back to work before they fire us," Gloria said.

An old inside joke the hospital auxiliary ladies had beat to death. No one could fire a volunteer.

"Okay, see you around." I waved and hurried out the revolving door. It didn't take me long to get half way across town to the house, where I ran inside, grabbed my old uniform jacket off the hanger, and changed. No one would question a volunteer's appearance on any floor. They escorted patients and their visitors all over the place.

I smoothed down the sleeves, straightened the front buttons, which had grown a little tight, and tucked the divorce papers inside the waistband, along with the ball-point pen. I planned to strike and run before he knew what hit him. That should impress Mr. Levine.

When I went by the entry way, I spied George's extra set of keys hanging from the little bronze key hook. He had a thing about not messing up the line of his clothing with a key bulge in his pants pocket and only carried the keys on his person when he had to. So irrevocably finished—his need for keys. I probably should take them upstairs and put them with his other keys, but the thought made me sad.

At the hospital, I hurried up the back steps and grabbed a utility elevator. No need to take a chance of running into Gloria or Alice.

On the fourth floor, I stopped at the nurse's station. "Could you tell me where I might find C. C. Patterson? I have a message for him."

The nurse on call frowned and looked at the duty sheet. "He'd probably be mopping at the end of the hall. He goes on a break in ten minutes." She pointed down the hallway, her finger curved left.

"Uh…how will I know him? Does he wear a badge with his name?"

The nurse shook her head. "Doesn't have to. Not many seven foot men work on the floor."

I felt my mouth dry out. Seconds ago my main thoughts had been relatively simple. Should I wait for his break and follow him into the employee lounge or accost him in the hall? Just how much against this divorce was he? Would anyone really harm a motherly looking hospital volunteer? I took time out to curse Mr. Levine under my breath too, while I was at it. He probably knew all about Mr. Patterson, and was getting a big fat yuk out of this.

I straightened my shoulders and sucked in my stomach. I needed this job to hire a PI to help me. George's reputation, his retirement, my life might be in danger if George had been murdered—a lot was at stake here.

Suddenly, before I could prepare for it, I nearly ran into C.C. Patterson. There was no mistaking him, not in a crowd of thousands. He was a very tall black man.

We stood alone in a long, narrow hallway. All the hospital room doors were closed, leaving nowhere to go but forward.

"Mr. Patterson?" My voice began in a squeak, and I managed to lower it when I cleared my throat.

He didn't speak, but turned to stare at me. He looked like a wrestler or a boxer, in magnificent shape. The drab green uniform did nothing to hide his bulging muscles. Oh God, did I want this job bad enough to die for it? I got a sudden flash of him stomping my body into the shiny terrazzo floor or shoving my head down into that milky white bucket of Pine-Sol.

Before I could turn and run, I whipped out the papers and handed him the pen. "I need you to sign this." It was my best PTA board voice, as firm and authoritative as I could manage under the circumstances.

He had to have heard me swallow through a pitifully dry throat when he obediently reached for the paper and accepted the pen. He leaned it against the wall and scribbled his name on the bottom line. I prayed the ink in the ball-point pen wouldn't freeze up at the angle of his writing.

Handing it back to me, he smiled, but his eyes were sad. "Been expecting this. No use avoiding it anymore." He picked up the bucket and mop and walked away.

My legs refused to hold me much longer. I wobbled to the first room with an empty bed and hurried inside to sit on the chair by the door. I took several deep breaths, the sweat felt icy down the center of my back.

But I had done it.

Chapter 7

The next morning, I triumphantly placed the signed affidavit on Mr. Levine's desk. He looked at me over his half glasses. The brief flicker of surprise in his stare told me he *had* known about Mr. Patterson.

That, apparently, was all the satisfaction I was going to get from him. He shoved another manila envelope toward me.

It was then I noticed a man sitting in the back office using the phone, his chair tilted against the wall, his feet up on Mr. Levine's desk. When he hung up, he winked at me through the open door, and I smiled in response, something I would normally never do. I tarried a moment, reluctant to leave.

He sauntered out of the room, hands in his pockets.

"Hi there." The man had a pleasantly deep voice that went along with his tall, lanky frame and his pleasant appearance. He wasn't handsome in the way that George had been, but his features were arranged well and his smile was dazzling.

"Hey, you still here?" Levine said in his normally charming growl. It didn't faze the stranger.

"Haven't seen you around," the man said. He was looking at me.

Before Mr. Levine got a chance to tell him I was a lowly employee, I stuck out my hand. "Edwina Hartley."

"Jake Dugan. I'm the PI from next door."

"Yeah, and if you'd pay your phone bills on time, you wouldn't have to park your ass in here," Levine groused, but I could tell his heart wasn't in it. Mr. Dugan had to be something special to gain Levine's respect.

"I stopped by the other day and your office was closed," I said. There was this strong urge to confide my suspicions to some kind of professional person before talking myself out of them. Some inner voice warned me against going to the police yet.

"Sure, doll, come on over to my office. Thanks, Harry."

Mr. Levine's frown let me know our business was finished. With the manila folder tucked under my arm, I followed the PI out the front door and into his office.

Mr. Dugan towered over me. He had to be about six foot, although most everyone seemed taller compared to my five feet, three inches. He was lean as a greyhound and walked with an angular grace.

His office was small, but neat and Spartan, compared to Mr. Levine's. No smelly used milk containers or discarded pizza boxes lying about in this room.

He pulled out a chair for me and sat behind the desk. I waited for him to lean back and clasp his hands behind his head like every PI on television had ever done. He just looked at me and asked, "What can I do for you?"

Where to begin? Fern would have been better at explaining, she was a great one for details, but since she wasn't with me, I knew I'd better get on with it. "My late husband—I think he was murdered," I blurted.

His smile disappeared and a frown appeared between his eyes. I had his attention.

"I'm listening."

I told him about the gambling, about the veiled threats over the phone from the bookies, about the bloodstains.

"Hmm. There could be a logical explanation for the blood. A bookie doesn't normally kill off his source of income, no matter how annoyed he is. He might break— ah—warn the customer, but kill? Uh, uh. Wouldn't take long to run out of clients at that rate."

Okay, so Fern was right. Big deal. "It hurts me to think of it, but maybe someone used a needle. There wasn't much blood."

"Didn't the medical examiner check it out?"

"There was only George's doctor and the hospital doctor. I haven't had the courage to really *look* at the medical report yet, but George had diabetes and heart problems. I'm pretty sure his doctor listed heart failure as reason for death."

"Where'd you say the stain was?"

"Almost at the top of his right arm."

"Hmm. Not normally where a diabetic person would give himself a shot."

"I don't suppose so, but George took pills, not shots. Are you sure there wasn't some terrible weapon used?" I hoped not so hard, my face felt frozen, waiting.

"Nope. You mentioned there was only a drop of blood on the pajamas and the chair. In the first place, there would have been more blood, which the doctors wouldn't have missed. Anyway, the blood stain would be in the chest area, most likely. If someone killed your husband, they could have done it with a needle filled with something." He looked pensive. "Something that wouldn't leave a trace within hours."

"But if not a bookie, who would want to kill him?" I voiced my puzzlement in a shaky manner that had me clearing my throat.

He leaned forward. "Did your husband have a large life insurance policy? I'd bet so."

"Well, at one time he did."

He didn't question my use of "one time" and I was glad. That was an embarrassing thing to admit, that my loving husband had canceled our insurance.

"What were you doing the night he died?"

"What?"

"The police will ask if we start digging."

I felt encouraged. He did say "we." It was hard to keep dredging up that night over and over. "I went to a book discussion at the library."

"Is this a regular thing? Did you stay to the end?"

"It's every other Wednesday, and I usually stay for the full three hours. But this book wasn't to my liking, and I cut out at first break and went home. Oh, I stopped off at the store and picked up some of George's favorite ice cream."

"Hmm. Anyone notice you, talk to you?"

I wished he'd quit humming. It sounded ominous. "Probably no one noticed me. No one spoke beyond the usual hellos or nods at the library. I don't know any of them. It's not like a group or anything. The individuals change, depending on the book involved. I arrived a little late, sat in the back, and left early."

He leaned his elbows on the desk and folded the tips of his long fingers together like a tent, regarding me with steady interest.

"Are you saying that I might be a suspect? That's terrible. I loved George, and he loved me."

"Did you say your husband *had* a large insurance policy?"

"Well, I guess you might say that. Until he cashed it

in or borrowed on it extensively to pay his gambling debts."

I appreciated his wince. "You didn't find that out until after he died, did you?"

"No. I see what you're getting at. The police might think I was tired of his gambling and decided to cash him in."

The first smile. It was electric. He had a tiny dimple on one side of his cheek. "Could be their first thought. They like to wrap up a murder soon as they can. Most time, a family member or a friend is involved."

"Like I said before, there wasn't any reason to think George died from anything other than a heart attack. His diabetes surely didn't kill him. His doctor was there and signed the papers."

"Did you call it in to nine-one-one?"

"Yes. I told them I thought my husband had had a heart attack. Then I called his doctor." Tears edged against the corners of my eyes, and I willed them to stay back. I never cried in front of strangers.

"You could go down to the precinct, check their records. There wouldn't be much. Also get a copy of the hospital records. Were you with him there?" He played with a pencil, tapping it on the desk.

"Of course. The doctor and I followed in the car. They wouldn't let me ride in the ambulance."

"Did they give him oxygen or use the electric paddles on him or try CPR?"

I shook my head. "No, I don't think so."

"Okay. Want me to check it out for you?" He pulled forward in his chair to stare into my eyes. "Are you willing to accept the fact that your husband's body might have to be exhumed if you pursue this?"

"Maybe. I suppose so. If someone murdered George in his own home, I can't let that go unpunished, can I?"

"No. It could put you at risk, though. If someone killed your husband, it was for a reason, and the same people won't want you stirring the pot. On the other hand, it may not be necessary to bring up the body. You say he had diabetes. If someone knew that, for example, shot him with a loaded insulin syringe, that would put him in a coma, and he would die. But the insulin leaves the body within hours."

The thought of George subsiding into a coma made my stomach clench painfully, and I pushed away the idea. George never reacted well to pain or sickness. "I didn't know that. There is one problem with paying you. I—I haven't a lot of money at my disposal. The bank will take back the house. I can sell my furniture, or most of it. There's a little more you should know."

He waited, as if he had already figured that out.

"Did I mention the company where my husband worked as an accountant thinks he may have embezzled about fifty thousand dollars?"

The look on his face told me I'd forgotten to mention that little item.

When he sighed and leaned back in his chair, eyes closed, I knew he made an effort to recover the Mr. Cool image he obviously worked so hard to perfect. "Anything else you're leaving out?"

"No. I don't think so."

"Do *you* believe he embezzled?"

Strange question. What did it matter? I shook my head. "No. George gambled and never told me, I'll admit that. But he looked forward to his retirement. Maybe that was why he took a chance and cashed in his insurance policies. Figured with the money from his retirement, he'd get the policies going again."

"Hmm."

"As I started to say, I don't have a lot of ready cash. That's why I'm working for Mr. Levine—"

"What?" He leaped out of the chair and, before I knew it, he'd rounded the desk and pulled me to my feet. I didn't even have time to protest before he dropped my arm and looked sheepish. "Sorry. Got carried away. I just can't believe Harry would take advantage of a lady of your…ah…obvious distinction. Are you sure you know what working as a process server involves?"

He may have been in his fifties, not more than five years younger than me. It felt odd that he looked at me so respectfully. But no one was going to take charge of my life again, telling me what I could or could not do.

I tilted my chin in the air and glared at him. Hard to do with him looming over me. "I've already completed one difficult assignment without problems," I said stiffly. No need to tell him about my lack of qualifications on the job market. He probably already figured that out too.

He snorted and turned away to stare at the wall a long moment. I gathered my purse and stood, waiting. I needed his expertise, but it was hard asking for help.

"Okay. Let's play it this way. You get paid, you can pay me."

"That seems fair. Thank you. What if I start checking out things by going to the firm, asking to remove George's personal effects from his office? He might have left something behind, some clue about the embezzlement deal."

He frowned. "I don't know about that. Someone in the firm could have set your husband up as a fall guy. You know, to take the heat off the real embezzlers?"

"That hardly makes sense. When an employee dies or leaves, the corporation calls in an outside auditor automatically. They wouldn't want that to happen." I thought of the two men from the company who came to visit me. They hadn't mentioned an outside investigator until I brought it up. Why did they come to my house instead of calling me into the office? Were they searching for something? Or sizing things up to investigate later? That Jordan character would certainly be capable. He had a cold, hard look in his eyes.

"Hasn't the company sent George's personal effects home yet?"

"No. They told me a messenger would bring them to me. I asked them to wait a while." It was too soon to tackle that aspect of George's life what with the closets to go through and dresser drawers filled with his belongings.

"Know anything about computers?"

"A little. George tried to show me how to play Mahjong…you know, that little game with tiles and—"

He waved away my explanation, and waited.

"We have one in the den. He brought work home sometimes."

"Okay. We can check that out anytime. If he has one in his office, and if you go there again, look for little objects the size of a pinky finger. They're called thumb drives sometimes. Or he may have saved information on a CD. If it was important, it wouldn't be lying around. If they haven't locked it, turn on his computer and look for some obscure file that might be overlooked. Hopefully, he didn't have a personal password. Most companies won't allow that. Check the desk drawers, take them out if you can or feel underneath for anything taped. He might have hidden information and didn't get a chance to bring it home."

"You mean George might have known someone was trying to frame him?" The idea made my skin crawl, to think of George, fearful for his life, perhaps, and keeping it to himself. More and more, I had the sinking feeling that I'd been living with a stranger for many years. Did that make our life together a waste of time? Had I muddled up so many years of my life? But I loved George, and I knew he loved me. That had to count for something, even if we were not exactly "soul mates."

"He didn't mention problems at work or with an employee?"

I felt my face flush with embarrassment. How to explain? "George never discussed his work. When we met, he taught as a college professor, and I was one of his students. I suppose we never went beyond that mind set." Long, long ago, George and I had lain in bed half the night talking. What had happened in the meantime?

"Not even chit-chat? Office gossip? Anything might be important."

"No. George wasn't much for chit-chat. We were married a few years before our son was born. As soon as George found out about the baby, he quit the college and went to work for Graham, Graham, and Wilbur Accounting, in spite of my arguments against it. I believed he had deeply embedded his life in the staid, crusty halls of learning. But he wanted to earn a better living for his family. He gave up his life's work to provide me with possessions I never asked for nor wanted. That's so sad." I took a deep breath, having said it all at once. No pulling the Band-Aid off slowly.

"So…"

"So, I'm saying I don't have the foggiest notion of what George did on a daily basis. I've been to company parties and met most of the employees and supervisors on his floor. He never wanted to mingle with them personally, though. Felt it was inappropriate."

I had to face facts. George had been a stubborn, self-centered prig and, all the while, pretending to do everything for my benefit. He had *wanted* the job at the corporation. If anyone with George's personality could be said to blossom, he did so when he joined GG&W. I'd never thought of it before, I'd always carried the yoke of guilt around on my shoulders, thinking he'd given up so much for me.

"You okay?"

I caught his concerned expression full on and it came so unexpected it nearly did me in. "Yes. I'm fine. Just…you know…memories flash back at times."

He nodded without speaking.

Good. It would have been impossible to accept the intrusion of sympathy at that moment. "I have to go now."

He stood close, bending his head to peer into my face, raising his hand as if wanting to pat my shoulder, but he didn't touch me. Instead, he opened the door.

"Don't poke around too much, and I know you'll use discretion. I'm not going to lie to you, there could be something going on here, and amateurs only muck things up. Maybe the whole thing with your husband is easily explainable, maybe he did embezzle, maybe…ah, well, you get the drift. But I'll do what I can, starting with the hospital records." He retrieved a card from his desk.

I fished in my purse for George's card showing our phone number.

"Be careful and, above all, keep quiet about your ideas, at least until we can get a handle on this. George won't be going anywhere. You can afford to be patient."

Indeed, George wouldn't be going anywhere, but I'd lay odds, if I were a betting person, he was turning somersaults in his grave by now.

Chapter 8

Oh, sweetie, are you sure you want to do this? There must be some way you can get some money. I wish to God we could loan you some to tide you over, but with two kids sent through college, we never managed to save a dime."

"I wouldn't think of it, Fern. While you and Joe were scrimping to make ends meet, George was living it up and dragging me with him all the way. You mustn't feel guilty. Besides, it's a challenge, and I need that."

"When do you think the bank will repossess?"

I reached to smooth back a wisp of bangs on her forehead. Her straight brown hair that she kept in a pony-tail sometimes didn't all come together neatly.

"I have no idea. I didn't think it was necessary to mention George's death to them, they surely have discovered it by now. When the monthly payments stop, they'll notice. I put an ad in the paper for the Hepplewhite credenza. I thought just one item at a time would be better than having the yard sale that I threatened."

"Good idea," Fern said. "That way those creeps who are calling you might not get a way into your house."

"Darn! I hadn't given that a thought!" We sat in the back yard on the bench near one of George's prize rose bushes. The smell overpowered me, and I started to sneeze violently. Was he trying to tell me something?

"Didn't you say Junior had made a small portfolio for you? What about that money?"

I shrugged. "At the time, I wasn't sure of my...my financial acumen and put the account in both Junior's and my names. I can't touch it without Junior's knowing and asking questions."

"Lordy, lordy. I had no idea you were so..."

"Clueless? Cozy in my little cocoon? Go ahead and say it. I've chastised myself enough since George left me. My parents managed their lives together in the same way, so I just thought it was fine. And it was until—"

"Oh, my dear, I wouldn't put those names on you. If George had a safety deposit box, you could get to the bank before they know. It won't be sealed yet."

I squared my shoulders and met her eyes. "He never told me about any of our finances. I left that all up to him. He was an accountant, remember?"

That stumped her for a long moment, and her brow

wrinkled, her mouth puckered, and I almost felt sorry for her predicament. Until I realized it wasn't her skinny butt on the line here.

Then she rallied. "Yes, and even if your mother did the same with your father, honey, you don't have any options of sticking your head in the sand anymore. I bet if we check out his study, he'll have put some information aside. In a book or on his computer."

"Maybe. First thing though, I've got to get down to George's office today. Before they move everything." I'd told her about the detective's suggestions. "I decided not to call for an appointment, just surprise them."

"Now that's ballsy. Need any company?"

"No, I'd better go alone. I don't want them to think I'm looking for something special."

"And what would that be?"

"I'm not sure. Records George may have stashed away. A key taped under a desk drawer, maybe a computer gizmo hidden."

Fern looked properly impressed. No need to tell her Dugan had come up with most of these ideas.

That afternoon, when I arrived at the accounting firm, I took an elevator up to George's floor. In the hallway, at the entrance to the suite of offices I saw a bronze sign on the wall stating that only persons in possession of a pass card were allowed to enter except by previous appointment.

I had an inkling this might happen. George showed

me his pass card long ago. Did they change anything when an employee left? Maybe they'd forgotten they hadn't asked for his card back.

Delving into the bottom of my purse, my fingers touched George's wallet. I'd started carrying it around with me, since it contained all the cards that confirmed him a valid member of society like his social security card, cards for health insurance, life insurance, credit cards, and a card stating that he'd had cataract surgery with implants.

Inserting the corporate card into the slot, I held my breath until the door swooshed open. The vestibule was empty, and the receptionist desk ahead of me had no one behind it. I knew which way to George's office. Did I dare try it?

Common sense took over my sudden inspiration. If they caught me, I'd be thrown out summarily. And the wrong person might guess I was searching for something. But if I innocently asked to pack up my husband's belongings, could they refuse?

I marched up to the receptionist area and plunked my purse loudly on the desk. Heads all over the room turned in my direction when I caught everyone with a surprised look. This was their inner sanctum, safe from outsiders.

"Yes?" The receptionist's voice came cold and clipped when she walked up to the desk, but she was too cool to ask how I got in and why. I'd have to give her that information soon enough.

"I'm Mrs. George Hartley."

Her look stayed blank, as if pasted on her face. Maybe it was permanent.

"The late Mr. Hartley. He was an employee here until recently."

Like for twenty-three years, sister. How long have you worked here? I kept quiet, remembering why I didn't bring Fern.

"Oh. Yes. I'm so sorry about your loss, Mrs. Hartley. We all enjoyed working with Mr. Hartley so much." Her smile went as far as the first crow's feet under her makeup and stopped abruptly. "How can we help you?" She looked pointedly at the card I still held in my hand. I knew it was only a matter of a few sentences between us before she asked for it.

"Mr. Jordan told me I was welcome to come clean out my husband's personal effects." I hoped Jordan didn't work on this floor. "I brought plastic grocery bags to carry the belongings home with me," I added, flashing the folded bags in an effort to prove that I was only a dumpy housewife on a lonely mission of love.

"Perhaps I should verify—"

"I don't think that's necessary," I interrupted. "Mr. Jordan probably is out to lunch now anyway." It was nearing noon, I'd picked that time deliberately thinking a lot of the office staff would be out.

"Well…"

I held my breath while she debated. When she nodded toward the corridor in the direction of George's office, I knew I'd won. Temporarily.

When she let me inside the room, I had to swallow hard. Faint traces of George's aftershave still lingered, and I could feel his presence. I didn't bother to hide the tears in my eyes when I turned to her. "Do you mind closing the door? I'd like to be alone with...with his things for a while."

To her credit, her botoxed face expressed as much sympathy as possible. She touched my shoulder briefly then backed out and closed the door.

'*Hurry—hurry.*' George's aftershave swirled around me, pushing me to action. The computer and all the electronic gizmos were unplugged, and I had no idea how to put it all back together, so I just touched the little button I'd seen George use to make the machine light up. Nothing did.

I slid open the long shallow drawer on his desk and touched the supplies so neatly laid out. George had been a neatnik to the extreme. Exquisitely sharpened yellow pencils lay sorted by length and one eraser, looking as if it had never been used, had its own niche. The third drawer was different. Opening it, I fingered through the misplaced pens and paper clips. George had stapled little notes together but now they lay crumpled and scattered over the top of the contents to the rear of the drawer. Not like George. Someone had been here, messing up his things, looking for something too.

I felt under the drawers, but my fingers touched nothing that stuck out. I got down on my hands and knees and crept underneath the desk, searching. I pulled each drawer out and felt all over them. A glance at my watch said time was flying by. Soon lunch hour would be over and someone would surely come to see how I was doing. I doubted they had forgotten me.

When I stood, my image reflected from the gold-webbed mirror across the room. My hair was a mess, standing straight up in places. I'd ruined a pair of new panty hose, but luckily my skirt was calf-length and the runs wouldn't show.

"Dummy!" I whispered to the image staring back at me. "What do you care about that now? Don't get your knickers in a roll." Staring so hard at the mirror, I noticed a tiny bit of white paper showing at the upper edge. Pulling the chair across the room wasn't hard, but my heart pounded anyway. I climbed onto the chair and balancing one foot perilously on the arm, reached for the paper. It didn't budge, although the mirror was set a little ways away from the wall by hidden studs.

Damn! What now? If I didn't check this out now, they'd never let me back in here, bet on that one, George.

Luckily I'd taken the precaution of locking the door. The knob rattled and the receptionist's voice came through muffled.

"Mrs. Hartley. Is everything all right in there?"

"Yes, of course. I...I locked the door because…because I needed privacy. This isn't easy." I managed an audible sniffle.

A long pause, I got down off the chair in case she had a key with her.

"Let me know when you've finished. I have to go to lunch, but I'll wait for you."

Bad luck. That put the pressure on me and this was going to take some doing. After all that, the paper might turn out to be a part of the mirror peeling off.

I spied a taller, stronger chair across the room and, pushing the other flimsy thing aside, I dragged the big chair closer. It took a few minutes of prying with a nail file retrieved from my purse, but the white paper finally came out wrapped around a small gizmo that Dugan had described as a thumb drive.

I sat down on the nearest chair and opened the paper. Even prepared as I was, it struck me that this might have been one of the last things George had written. Tears blurred my eyes and I wiped them away with impatience, trying to read the neat, concise printing. It made no sense to me. Numbers followed numbers, but not in any sort of series.

The door rattled again, a serious rattle that said time was up. I pushed the note and drive into my purse, and then on second thought, tucked it inside my bra. My blouse was loose enough not to give me the outline of having an odd-sided boob, I hoped.

I grabbed up the meager lot of George's belongings

and stuffed them into the plastic grocery bags I'd brought along. Talk about class, George would have been mortified.

"Okay, I'm finished," I called out as I hurried to let her in.

It wasn't a her. It was the devil's duo, Mr. Jordan and Mr. Carroll. They stood, arms akimbo, blocking my exit.

"I came to clean out George's personal possessions," I said unnecessarily.

Mr. Jordan might have imagined he smiled but it was more like a slight twitch of his lips. His eyes looked dark and cold as a winter night. They maneuvered me back inside and closed the door behind them with a quiet click that sounded ominous in the sudden silence of the room.

I held the bags toward them. "Would you like to inspect these to see if I took a stapler by accident?"

Carroll, the smaller, younger one, shook his head. At least he had the grace to look embarrassed. "We would have done this for you, Mrs. Hartley. You shouldn't have had to put yourself through this."

"Thank you. It was another way of bidding my husband goodbye. Of getting some closure." Did I really dab at my eyes? I laid the bags down on the desk. The two men exchanged glances.

"We may have left you with the wrong impression, Mrs. Hartley. George was a valuable, trusted employee until—ah, his little misstep. However, we do not mean to cast aspersions on *your* character."

What a pompous ass. If George did make off with the money, I wouldn't have blamed him. Having to work with people like Jordan and Carroll for twenty some years couldn't have been a life's dream after all. Had there come a time when this truth came home to haunt him? Poor George.

"How soon will it be before the special accountants go over the books to tell me when I will receive George's pension? I probably should get our personal attorney to look into this matter." I hadn't contacted him about any of my problems because he basically was George's attorney, and I'd always thought he looked down his nose at me.

"You may do so, of course. But it would be an additional expense for you and could cause unnecessary publicity reflecting on George's...ah...gaming proclivities. I assure you we are handling the alleged embezzlement with the utmost discretion. We see no need to bother the authorities if we are able to recoup the funds through George's retirement benefits."

What did that mean in simple English? Who would decide if George was guilty? I had a feeling the retirement benefits were water under the bridge either way.

Carroll handed me the bags and did not deign to peek inside. They opened the door and escorted me to the outer area, whereupon Jordan held out his hand. Instinctively, I knew it wasn't for a shake.

I reached into my purse to retrieve the card key.

He pocketed it and Carroll walked me out. We remained silent on the ride down the elevator and he touched his finger to his forehead in a gesture of farewell as I left the building.

After hailing a cab, thoughts bombarded me all the way home, my mind a jumble of disjointed ideas and perceptions. In my heart of hearts, I did not believe George to be a thief. Still, why did he hide the little drive, and what did the numbers mean? If George *had* stolen the money and deposited it in a Swiss bank account, why would there be three sets of numbers and not one? I was sure Fern would know all about Swiss bank accounts from watching her soaps. And the PI should know about them.

Those corporate barracudas were not going to get their hands on George's retirement without a fight. That I needed it to live on was beside the point. George had worked twenty years at a job I now knew he had ended up hating, and I felt somehow responsible. Had *they* had anything to do with his death? The thought made my legs weak, and I was glad to be sitting down in the taxi.

It was like a snowball ride downhill with the snow growing so big it threatened to engulf me. Would I end up dead like George?

Just as I was getting out of the cab, I realized that I'd forgotten to move the heavy chair back in place by the window in the office. My mind went back to the definite marks on the carpet where the tall chair had been. Would they notice?

If I were a betting person, I'd bet on it.

Chapter 9

Once in the house, I locked the door behind me and ran to the computer in the den. I "booted it up," as George was fond of saying, and put in the little drive. The light came on the screen and it asked for a password. Now what should I do? I touched a few keys on the keyboard but they didn't show on the screen and nothing else happened.

He must have had a password as Dugan mentioned. I searched his desk and wastebasket looking for anything that could be a password and then chided myself. George wouldn't have a paper like that lying around. He would have memorized it.

Taking out the drive, I turned off the computer and looked around for a good hiding place. The back of the Cezanne painting. Who would think to look there? No, that was dumb. I'd have to take it off the wall soon and try to sell it at one of the galleries. As far as I knew it was an original, George hadn't tolerated reproductions of anything.

I knelt down and pulled up a corner of the carpet under the desk. The front where the chair sat was covered with a thick plastic. I couldn't imagine anyone crawling around looking for something there. I put the papers George had written the figures on in a brown envelope and slipped it underneath quite a ways. Now if I could remember where I hid it.

I stashed the drive thingy in one of the zipper compartments in my purse. There were so many damn zippers in that bag, anyone would have a problem searching through it. It would have been good to talk to Fern. She might be home by now, but I had to sort some things out alone.

ొఎ౿ఎ

The next morning, the president of the bank holding our mortgage called on the phone, opening his conversation with polite reserve. "Edwina. Did you receive our flowers? A small token of our regard for George."

So they did know. The flowers were probably on their way. "Thank you, Sean. What a lovely tribute." I waited, not taking pity on his unusual hesitation.

"Are you aware George canceled the rather expensive death insurance on the mortgage?" He harrumphed in that way he had when I trumped him at bridge.

"How could that be?" I asked. "Isn't that a requirement for a mortgage?" I could feel his head shake over the phone, imagining cash register noises going off inside his bald pate. The thought brought me a mild twinge of amusement which quickly dissipated with his next words.

"No, not after a certain amount of years into the mortgage. This is hard for me to say, Edwina. I'm wearing two hats, and this one is not your bridge partner speaking. As president of the bank, I have certain odious duties."

He cleared his throat again and I almost felt sorry for him. It wasn't his fault George had made this mess. Immediately, I felt ashamed. George didn't kill himself either or ask to be murdered. "Okay, Sean. Let me have the gory details."

"The bank must insist you either keep up the mortgage payments, or we will be forced to foreclose."

The next thing he would probably tell me, George was behind with his payments.

"I'm afraid the bank—actually, I have, as a friend—been allowing George certain latitude with his account. You are, in effect, six months in arrears. My career, as I know it, will be in serious jeopardy, not to mention my retirement."

Tell me about it. I sat very still, hoping a stray bolt of lightning would find its way down and put me out of my misery. "How much time do I have?" I managed to croak out.

At first, I didn't think he heard me and then he spoke, his voice dry and clipped. "As a friend, I have to advise you to vacate as soon as reasonable unless—"

It was my turn to shake my head. "No, there's no unless, Sean. Everything is gone, looks like."

"Frances and I—we could loan you a bit to tide you over. On a personal level, of course," he offered.

"Thanks, that's kind of you. But right now it would be a waste." Fern would have said it would be like peeing on a four alarm fire. I'm just so sorry we caused you problems."

"Have you begun to make plans?"

"I don't know what I'm going to do, but I'll try to make it as easy on you as I can."

After hanging up, I looked longingly toward the table in the dining room where I'd been sitting to have my cries. I didn't have the luxury of a pity party right now. Maybe later when I had time to collapse.

I rummaged through George's briefcase and withdrew a yellow legal pad. That seemed very efficient. I'd take inventory of the salable possessions before I lost the roof over my head.

The contents of George's briefcase carried the lingering scent of his peppermint breath fresheners he was always chewing and a wave of sorrow overcame me, so that I sat down quickly. "George, I hope you're happy where you are. I even hope you can't see what you left behind. Or didn't leave," I amended. I spoke the words out loud and pulled the tissue from my sleeve to wipe away my tears.

When I touched fingers lightly over the yellow pad, I felt indentations of writing. I'd never know what possessed me to go through the desk to find carbon paper. That was almost a Fern-thing. But I did, and when I rubbed the blue carbon paper over the pad, numbers leaped out at me. Were they the same numbers on the list from George's office?

I knelt and pulled out the envelope of papers under the carpet. Side by side the numbers matched with the exception of one extra number followed by a period and three initials. Dot *txt*, I knew that much about computer language—no one called the dots periods. Now, what in the world could that mean?

Taking off the top yellow sheet and folding it into a manageable square, I stuck that in the envelope too and slid it under the carpet again. Sooner or later I'd have to find a better hiding place, but the paper wouldn't bulge under the short napped Persian carpet.

After I had another cup of coffee to steady my nerves, I called Dugan, who wasn't in. Next, I called Fern, who came right over.

We spent some time drinking coffee while I told her about my office visit. I could tell she was impressed with my *chutzpah*, as Mr. Levine might have put it. I wasn't ready to start on the other job I'd gotten from him just yet, so I thought it a good time to get started on an inventory of the furnishings with Fern's help.

"Aren't you going to keep any of this?" Fern asked.

"Why? I don't even know where I'm going. Won't it look cute if I bring this credenza with me out on the street?"

"Bosh! You exaggerate. Joe and I'd never let that happen."

I tried to picture living with Fern, Joe, and all the visiting grandkids who popped in unexpectedly from time to time, not to mention their dog named T Rex, very aptly I thought. He didn't like visitors. A sensation of guilt washed over me. I shouldn't be ungrateful for what a good friend offered. Living on the streets seemed more inviting, but at least Fern had tried to cheer me up.

"Do you know anyone with computer expertise?" I asked, trying to sound off-hand.

Fern had been sitting at the grand piano, touching the keys lightly, more like searching for dust. She and Mr. Clean would have been soul mates. "Joe has a friend, believe it or not, a computer nut. He helps the guys set up their laptop when they buy one and fixes it when they crash."

Joe and Fern never got into computers—they were both computer-phobic. I shuddered to imagine Fern let loose on Facebook or Twitter. I guess I wasn't curious, even though I'd watched George pecking away at the keyboard some nights when I didn't have anything better to do.

I wondered if he'd had access to bookies on the computer. That would have been way too easy for him.

"Why do you want to know about computers all of a sudden?" Fern asked.

"I found some numbers hidden away in George's office. I don't know what they mean but I'm sure they're connected to computers in some way."

Fern's skinny eyebrows shot up. "Maybe they're Swiss bank accounts. You might have some money around after all." Her voice rose in excitement. "Let me see them." She hopped off the piano bench and did a little impatient jig.

Before she could work herself into a tizzy, I retrieved the papers and handed them to her.

Her lower lip pushed up in that baby scowl that was all hers. "Nope, not a bank account," she said emphatically, handing the papers back to me.

"Well? Want to say why you're so sure of that?"

She always had to draw out any drama, milk it dry.

She smirked. "Last year in *Delightful Passage*, this very thing came up, and they showed an actual Swiss bank account. The numbers have to have letters before and after."

"Big deal. What makes you think your favorite soap knows everything?"

"Has to. They've a team of researchers on the payroll

all the time. You may have the right idea, this could be computer code."

"Maybe Dugan, the private investigator, will have an idea."

"You don't know him well enough to trust him too far," Fern reminded me.

If I was the good judge of character that I thought I was, I knew he could be trusted. But I saw no need to confide that feeling to Fern.

"I'm going to have to call George Two and tell him I may be moving."

"Guess so. But you might as well wait until the executor reads the will. And by the way, isn't it time you called him for an appointment? You said you asked him to wait until you called."

"You're right there. George should mention any safety deposit boxes he has. I asked Sean from the bank and he said there was one in George's name, but I'd have to get a court order to open it."

"Bummer. I guess I don't need to ask if you read a copy of the will already."

I shook my head, feeling really spineless. "No. I asked George once about what he wanted to happen at his demise and tried to tell him what *I* wanted, but he wouldn't talk about it. Said it was all arranged and not to worry."

Damn George! His unctuous consideration was turning into a velvet cage, and I felt much more trapped than when he was alive. At least *then* I didn't realize I was caged.

Fern gave a big sigh. "Well, at least you have some of the furniture—" She broke off when she saw me turn away.

Tears started and I wanted to give up right then and there, but how could I? *How does one give up, I mean, literally?*

She put her hand on my shoulder and pulled me into a hug. I sagged with the effort to stand on shaky legs.

"Tell me," she commanded.

"I found—I found bills in George's computer desk. He—he owed—he's maxed out on his cards. I'm afraid I don't own anything. If anything, I'll have to sell it all to repay the credit cards." Was I going to find out next that George had a mistress hidden away? But, no, how would he have had time for that? He was home every night punctually at six, and if we went out on weekends, we went as a couple. At least I had been spared that indignity.

Another big sigh from Fern. We sat on the couch, neither speaking. It was the first time I'd ever seen my friend speechless. I tried to enjoy the moment, but it wasn't possible.

"Let's look around," she finally suggested, leaping to her feet in that hyper way she had. "I bet he hid some cash somewhere."

"I guess we could look. But if I find money, that

might have to be saved to pay off the bookies."

"Nonsense. They'll leave you alone after a while."
She didn't sound that convinced, but I didn't argue.

We started upstairs. Each of us took rooms and first
went through all the drawers we could find.

"Don't forget to feel underneath," she yelled from
one of the side rooms, sounding as if she had her head
inside a drawer.

"I know, I know," I muttered. "I did that at George's
office, remember?"

*Save your bad temper for when it will do you some
good*, my inner voice cautioned.

"Bingo!" About thirty minutes had passed and Fern's
voice sounded triumphant coming from downstairs. I hurried down and she came through the doorway of the den
with a battered looking briefcase. Hardly something
George would have owned.

I took it from her, noticing it wasn't dusty at least.
"Where did you find this?"

"It was behind the television with a bunch of newspapers around it."

"What? George would never let any papers stay on
the floor for a moment."

"Well, it was there. Open it."

"Before we look, I should remind you if we find
money, it probably has to be paid on George's debts."

"Bull guano!" she exploded in anger. "For God's
sake, woman, they're taking the house and then the furni-

ture, don't you think that's payback enough? And to heck with the bookies, that's their tough luck."

I went into the living room, setting the ugly briefcase on the dining room table.

"Okay, you made your point. Now let's see what we have."

The case was locked and my fingers trembled when I tried to open it. Now what? I hurried into the kitchen and came back with a steak knife.

"Let's try this. Doesn't matter if we ruin the lock, does it?" When I heard the lock snap, I up-ended the case and a stack of bills fell out, held together neatly by a bank wrapper.

"Holy shit!"

Fern seldom swore and when she did, she looked as if she was waiting for someone to smack her. Catholic school upbringing, I figured.

She ruffled through the contents and began to count.

I was too impatient and broke the bank seal. After that we separated the new money into piles of $1,000 and stacked them so we could easily count.

Her eyes were big, and I thought mine must have been too when she totaled it to $100,000.

"I wonder why George hid this. Do you think he was going to split and leave for Tahiti or something?" I hadn't realized I'd spoken out loud until Fern snorted.

"No way! He had to have known he was digging himself in deep. Of course, gamblers always think they can gamble their way out of it, no matter how high it piles. Besides, he loved you—a lot. He would never pull out on you."

He did just that, I wanted to say, but it wasn't very satisfying to chastise someone *in absentia.* "Then what? I'm sure you have an idea."

"'Course I do. I think he figured someone was after him and he hid this away for you. Either that, or he was blackmailing someone. There may be more money." She lurched out of her chair and headed back to continue searching. When I didn't follow, she raised her eyebrows. "Coming? We got more looking around to do before they haul your furniture away."

Reluctantly, I followed her into another room. My feet felt heavy, like they were already encased in cement. Even this amount of money was a drop in the bucket. Where would I move? I looked around and suddenly the familiar home I hadn't paid much attention to looked so cozy. I felt enveloped in the arms of the house for the first time since we'd moved in.

*Too late, too la*te, a voice murmured in my head.

Chapter 10

We didn't find any more stashes of money in the rooms upstairs. I thought for sure we might find more tucked away in our bedroom where there must have been a gazillion hiding places. Did George regard that room's sanctity? I would have liked to hope so.

"Where do you suppose this money came from?" Fern asked.

"I suppose even gamblers like George have to win sometimes." That didn't convince me either.

Fern's forehead wrinkled, a momentous sign that she was thinking hard. "But what if—let's just say what if he was taking a payoff? Or blackmailing someone? What if he was blackmailing those suit and tie jobs from his office? Or—heaven forbid—he really embezzled the money."

I sighed. "Which reality news program is it this time?"

We were back in my bedroom, sitting on my bed, trying to figure out what I needed to take when I left the house. I couldn't pack all of the clothes—didn't even want them all. George had liked to pick out my clothes and most of them were his choices.

"That shows how much you know, girlfriend. I used to watch *America's Most Wanted*. But, actually, maybe one of my soaps *did* have a corporate blackmailer on the program once," Fern admitted. "They didn't call it that exactly. They called it...let's see...'manipulation of funds' or something to that effect."

"You don't leave me a pleasing picture of George. Gambler, blackmailer, funds manipulator. What's next? I'm only damn sure he didn't steal that money."

"I didn't *say* he was a blackmailer. Like you said, even gamblers win from time to time. He could have won and stashed the money away."

"And not pay off the bookies? He'd be smarter than that, I'd hope."

At Fern's raised eyebrow, I decided to let that one pass. In retrospect, George wasn't showing a great many smarts so far.

"All you have to do now, for the time being, is find a place to hide it. Don't tell me, I don't want to know."

I could hardly believe that, but I let it pass. I knew just where to hide it.

"So what's next? Will you be okay until you find out what the bank is going to do?"

"I've got enough put aside to rent a condo, what with first and last month's rent, utility deposits, and if it's somewhat furnished, I could get by for a month or two. That's not going to cut it, Fern." I wanted to curl up on the bed and pull the covers over my head, letting the angry, frightened, frustrated tears loose from deep inside my chest where they were building up a back-pressure. What would I do in a condo alone? Yet even with my closest friend, I couldn't allow myself to go to pieces. I'd wait until she left.

"There's a lovely mobile home park on the other side of town. Joe has friends who live there. We visited the other day, and I saw quite a few for sale signs up."

"A trailer park?" I felt my voice go up a notch and struggled to bring it back down, along with the volume.

"God, you sound like George Junior." Fern shook her head and even the bobbing little ponytail didn't make me smile.

"Oh, I don't mean to but—"

"Okay, so it's a step away from your mansion, but they're doublewides and beautiful inside and out. Furnished too. It's like a condo almost. You own the lot and pay the management to keep it up. That way you could manage a healthy down payment and then, if you're bound and determined to work for Levine, you'd be able to make payments."

"That's all well and good but—"

"You don't want to rent a condo or an apartment on this side of town, do you? Honestly? Wouldn't it be embarrassing to constantly run into the old crowd?"

I stared at the closets. I'd taken most of what I wanted out and thrown across the brocade love seat in the corner. It hadn't made a dent in what was left. And then there were George's clothing, some of which he'd never worn yet.

I could take a load to the Second Time Around Shop on consignment. It went against my grain, but I would need to scrape up pennies from now on. I was so thankful George had let me learn to drive finally.

Let me learn. What an odd phrase. Maybe that's what scared me most. I was on my own. Totally. There was no one to "let me" do anything. "I suppose we could look at—at a place to live. You *will* come with me, won't you?"

"'Course. Wouldn't miss it for the world. And if— I'm just saying if—anything needs tinkering with or fixing, Joe's good at that."

Tinkering or fixing—my thoughts turned more dismal. What did I know about running a house alone? The moment something malfunctioned, George called a plumber, or air conditioning person, or some other expert in to fix it. I lifted my chin and straightened my shoulders. I would learn. Like a new born chick coming out of a shell, I faced a whole new world, and I had to carry on.

Fern helped me pack suitcases of clothes, which she insisted on taking home for safekeeping.

"I don't want to involve you in this," I protested, but not too strenuously.

She echoed my thoughts. "Hey, did you stop and think George might not have paid for all your duds either? I can see you leaving your furniture behind, but we can't have you running around naked." She giggled at the idea.

We piled the clothing in Fern's SUV, and she hauled one load away to her house. I wanted to be alone to pack George's things. It was always a marvel to me, George's closet. Sometimes I just opened the doors and sat on the bed to look. He'd matched his suits, ties, shirts, and socks by colors and shades and hung them together on padded hangers. His shoes, highly polished, lay side by side under each garment he would wear them with. In the back of the closet, drawers with silk boxer shorts and additional socks lay in pristine condition, as if they'd never been worn.

My own closets were different. I threw my underwear, bras, and hosiery all together in drawers and none of my sports socks or knee-highs ever matched until I got the idea of buying them all in one color. For the first few years, George tried to keep us both tidy and then gave up on me. Did I do that on purpose, to keep my things private? I was not normally untidy. Thinking back, that must have been one of my silent rebellions. I wasn't sure all this introspection was good for the soul as they claimed. It certainly left a person wide open.

I checked all of George's pockets and never found even one race ticket. One particular item, his favorite baby blue cashmere sweater, did me in. I'd buried my face in the soft fabric, inhaling his after shave, when all the tears welled up at once. I sobbed until I didn't have breath anymore and then raised my eyes to apologize to George somewhere up there, for getting makeup and tears on his sweater.

I flopped back on the bed, the tears still rolling out of my eyes. I'd been concentrating so hard about what I was going to do that I hadn't really told George goodbye.

"Don't worry, George dear, I'll find out if someone killed you and make it right." I said the words out loud, hoping to stem the flow of tears that were exhausting me.

Somehow, I didn't feel as if his spirit was comfortable on the other side or even if it had gone over there yet. I was sure he must be worried about me, but George had always been singularly focused on rights and wrongs and justice. He'd want his murderers punished if that was the way he died.

And he would have been furious beyond words to know he wasn't getting his rightful retirement benefits posthumously. While I packed his clothes into giant yard bags, I realized that George was still pretty much in control of my life.

Chapter 11

After a long night of tossing and turning, I decided to take a taxi to Jake Dugan's office to see if the PI would really help me. When did I get so blasé that I could think of a private investigator as a PI?

A bell ringing downstairs interrupted my thoughts when I stepped out of the shower. I toweled off and let a caftan sink down over my head and drape my body, feeling weirdly exotic without taking time to put undies on. I rushed down the stairs, hoping at last someone would greet me with good news.

I should have known better. A strange man stood on the steps, and I do mean strange. He could have stepped out of the pages of *The Godfather*, if that hadn't been such a cliché.

We stood face to face a moment, neither of us speaking. Finally, I caved in. "Yes? May I help you?" I tried to force my voice into the prim, no-nonsense PTA mode, but it wavered on the end, giving me up.

He continued to stare and then his gaze roamed over the house and past my shoulder into the living area in a most insolent manner. In his prospective, I saw the white columns in front and the elegantly trimmed windows along with George's immaculate lawn.

I waited him out, tempted to slam the door in his face, but knew that wouldn't solve anything. He would probably stick those size twelves in the doorway.

Finally he spoke. "You George's missus?"

I nodded.

"Called you on the phone, ya know? Left messages."

"You didn't leave any number to call back." Not that I would have.

"No. I didn't." He looked as if he might want to push me aside and step into my living room. I couldn't have that. I pulled the door shut behind me and motioned to a white wrought iron bench covered with dark blue pillows, on the corner of the piazza. "Would you care to sit?"

He nodded and motioned me to go ahead.

When we were seated, he cracked his knuckles. To intimidate me or habit, I couldn't decide.

"George owed us big bucks. I was sent to…ah …appraise the situation."

The space between us wasn't very far, and I could feel my eyes trying to cross looking at him from such a close angle. That didn't give me the proper dignity I needed so I stood and looked down at him. "See this?" I waved at the house and garden. "It's going back to the bank. Including all our furniture and probably most of the clothes in my closet. I can't pay you anything, even if I thought that was fair. Which I don't. Your contract—or whatever you choose to call it—was with my husband. I had no knowledge of my husband's gambling proclivities until after his death."

The man sighed, looked down at his shoes, and rubbed his fingers across the bridge of his slightly askew nose. He looked to me like a caricature of a hoodlum, an ex-boxer who found an easier way to make a living.

I should have at least thought to bring the cell phone out with me in case I had to call 911, but that was dumb, he would have never let me get away with that. I looked out to the perimeter of our lawn; thick trees surrounded our place, giving George the privacy he loved. Hardly anyone ever made a turn in the cul-de-sac on the street in front of us.

I was trapped with whatever this man had in mind to do with me.

While my mind frantically searched out a weapon to use to defend myself on George's damned neat porch, the man's next words came soft and menacing.

"I don't believe you. George has been dealing with us for years. We got a—a profile on him. He's big in the community, has bank accounts, investments, insurance policies, you know? You may not think you owe us, but George's estate owes us. Big time."

I sat back down, my legs so weak that I could ignore sitting so close to him. It was hard confiding to a stranger the depths to which George had sunk before he died. But to save my life, I had to try.

When I finished telling him about the insurance policies and the six month arrears on our home and how the bank would foreclose any day, I paused and took a deep breath. "That's the God's honest truth. You can call his lawyer. You can ask the people he worked with. I can give you a number at the bank and the name of his banker. He'll tell you the truth if I give him permission." I threw up my hands and didn't bother to stop the tears trickling down my cheeks. Damn! I'd cried a lot lately. I hated that sign of weakness. "I don't know what to do myself, everything I knew is gone. My life is a lie. I have to move out of this—into a—a trailer park, for god's sake."

For a moment I thought he was going to pat my shoulder, but his eyes turned back cold again, and he stood to distance himself from me.

"I've heard all the sob stories. You won't believe it, but some are worse than yours. But we aren't running a non-profit business. We'll wait a reasonable time until you get things under control, but I will be back." He touched a finger to his forehead and turned away.

The silky purr of his car in the driveway let me know

he left, but I didn't stand to peer over the hedge to watch him go. It sounded like a Porsche. The neighbor on the corner had one and came up to the cul-de-sac to turn around sometimes. Maybe Fern was right. If I hid myself out in a neighborhood mobile home park, who would think to look for me there? It would give me time to do more checking around.

I decided it was time to pay Mr. Dugan a call, and halfway there I wondered if I should have checked to see if he was in the office, but when the taxi rolled to a stop at the curb, I saw a light in his window. I picked up the plastic bag with George's PJ tops as he'd requested. I hoped he wasn't looking for fingerprints because Fern and I had handled the garment repeatedly. That was how I'd found the drop of dried blood.

I opened the door to his office and a bell tinkled above the door. "Mr. Dugan, are you here?"

He appeared in the doorway, beckoned me to come in, and pulled a chair out across from his desk. "Morning. I've done a little investigating. Read the ME's report, checked into your husband's corporation." He'd paused as if finished.

"And?" I prompted.

He spread his finger together in that upward prayer looking manner, his eyes somber. "The ME's report and the hospital's told the same story of a heart attack. The corporation, though, that's another story. I've a snitch who's in with the mob, or what's left of it. He claims your husband's company is linked with mob money and laundering."

That stunned me into a long silence. Was George in on this? "Why haven't the authorities cracked down on them? Accountants have a lot of funds at their disposal or the ability to access accounts." I knew this from conversations I'd overheard between George and businessmen he spoke to at different functions.

"So true. But the feds, or whoever, won't make a move until they have all the information to make arrests. This business with George dying might have upset the whole operation."

"Could that be why the men in George's corporation are hoping to make the embezzlement charge stick? To take the heat away from the corporation?"

Dugan laughed. "You've been watching reruns of *Murder She Wrote*, have you? Heat? Charge stick? You surprise me."

Oh dear god, I was cloning Fern. I felt my cheeks redden. "That's so silly of me. I have this friend...well, she's hard to explain, but she talks like that a lot, and yes she is addicted to soaps and exposes."

His chuckle was infectious. "I'm kidding. It's okay. But you're right, that would explain why the corporation flunkies are so gung ho to smear George. They probably think of you as the little missus with plenty of insurance and a big house, which will keep you content and out of their hair."

He looked at the bag in my lap, and I stood to hand it over to him. "This is George's PJ top. If you want to see the spot on his chair you'll have to work fast. The bank will foreclose any day now."

His raised eyebrow let me know he thought I exaggerated. "I'm sorry to hear that. But meanwhile, I want to take a look at all the clothing." He gestured toward the bag. "I'll take a look at that later along with the chair. Have you rearranged anything since your husband's demise?"

"No, due to Fern's instructions, I haven't picked up the newspaper he was reading that night or touched his chair."

He grinned. "Smart lady, your friend. I hope to meet her."

"Oh, you will. She'll have to check you out sooner or later. By the way, I had a visit this morning." I told him about Bent Nose and our conversation.

He looked concerned for a moment, and I wondered if his expression was for me or the bookie. The cheap clock on his desk ticked loud in the silence.

"That's not good. But I don't think you're in any danger for the time being. If it's the Mafia, they're trying to keep low key now. I'm sure moving away will be traumatic for you, but it seems inevitable. Even *if* we get to the point where we find out that George was murdered and even who did it, chances are all you'll benefit from it financially with his retirement. If the corporation doesn't file a Form Thirteen, sooner or later, that is."

Didn't anyone ever have any good news to tell me? I felt like a dark cloud with lightning playing through it drifted along above my head, everywhere I went. At least I should get some rain out of it.

"Call your friend, ask her to come to your house, and I'll be there too. I want to hear from her what she thinks you should do and maybe get her take on all of this."

Fern wouldn't disappoint him. I was sure she would have a lot to say. I barely kept from confiding in him about the found money. There was time for that. "I should visit Mr. Levine for a minute," I said, looking toward the door. I'd chalked up a tidy sum on my last summons, actually my first and last so far, and I was eager to match wits with a new client. In the back of my mind, I probably needed a pat on the back from Levine but knew that would be a long time in coming.

"Not a good idea. Let me get a handle on this first. You'll have enough on your hands, packing and moving." He called a taxi and walked around the desk to take my hand. "I know you have a lot on your plate right now, but I figure you're a strong, resourceful person. Hang on to that idea."

I'd written my address on a piece of paper and left it on the desk. "When can I expect you?"

"The sooner the better. I'll be there in about an hour."

That was a comforting thought. I wanted to vacuum

the den and throw a cover over George's chair at the very least, until I did move. But of course, I didn't dare touch anything.

I could barely wait to tell Fern everything.

Chapter 12

Fern came right over, and we waited for Dugan. I told her about Bent Nose, even though I continued to wonder how much I dared confide in her. She might have a tendency to get excited about things like the Mafia or whoever they were, paying a personal call and threatening to come back later.

"So I'll finally get to meet your PI," she said, sipping her iced tea.

As if her words conjured him up, I heard the sound of tires on gravel, heralding someone entering the driveway. I stood to look, making sure it wasn't my hoodlum buddy returning, but the old dark blue Buick was certainly not a Porsche. I went out to greet him.

Fern, just about to lift the glass to her lips, turned and, bless her heart, didn't miss a beat. I poured glasses of tea all around. When Dugan lifted an eyebrow toward Fern, I said, without hesitation, "This is my friend, Fern.

Fern, this is the private investigator I was telling you about, Jake Dugan."

They shook hands.

"Quite a spread you have here," he commented.

"Yeah, and it's all going to disappear soon—poof!—like a puff of smoke," Fern said.

"We don't have to get into that, dear." I tried to shush her. I never felt comfortable airing my private life in front of strangers.

But there was no shushing Fern.

"I don't suppose she told you about old George kissing away the family fortune, did she?"

"Come on, it was no fortune to be sure," I remonstrated.

Dugan listened politely.

"It's true, Edwina, and if you're going to hire someone to help, why keep something from him that he may need to know? She's been threatened by bookies too. They found out where George lived and think this—"She waved her arm to indicate the house. "—is up for grabs to pay his gambling debts."

"Hmm. Interesting." He managed to get in a word when she ran out of breath finally.

"I believe I told him some of that," I said, not trying to hide my annoyance. Whose story was this anyway?

Fern sat back in her chair and lapsed into what she might have considered an apologetic posture.

"She's right of course. There's so much to tell you. I

did find a list in George's office, very well hidden, so it must be important. Fern claims they can't be Swiss bank numbers, which is what I thought. "

"Could be locker numbers. Some banks have accounts with just figures. Maybe a computer password. I'd like to take a look at your living room."

"We didn't touch anything," Fern said. "Well, maybe we did handle George's pajama top. But at the time, we didn't think of *murder*." She whispered the word theatrically.

Fern could never get enough drama in her life.

"It's okay to leave my car there unlocked? I see you have your property fenced in and gated."

"Yes, and she forgets to close the gate. That's how Broken Nose got in," Fern said, a bit self-righteously, I thought.

"Bent Nose," I corrected absentmindedly. I led the way and we all trooped inside the sliding glass door.

"I hate these things," he said, stepping over the threshold and pausing to touch the glass. He made a light circle with a finger by the side of the door latch. "Glass cutters, nothing to it and so silent you'd never hear a thing. They have a suction gizmo that lets down the cut out piece so it doesn't fall and break, making a noise."

Fine, just what I needed to hear. Of course, this was only the enclosed patio. The main door was huge with stained glass from top to bottom, "George had alarms installed."

"I never knew that," Fern spoke up.

"I thought, at the time, it was pretty paranoid of him after living here all these years to suddenly decide to worry about burglars, but you know George, once he got an idea. That's why I decided I didn't need the expense and—"

"You quit the alarm system?" both Fern and Dugan shouted at once.

By then, we'd reached the living room. I pointed to the chair. To take the spotlight off my apparently faulty reasoning. "He sat there and that paper was lying on the floor along with that couch pillow. George wouldn't have tolerated such disorder if he'd have been aware of it."

Dugan took out a magnifying glass from his jacket pocket to examine the top of the chair. "Hmm. I see the tiniest speck of what could be blood. Easy to miss if you aren't looking for anything. Did you say your husband had diabetes?"

Fern was sitting primly on the couch, like a child trying to stay invisible so she wouldn't be asked to leave the room.

"Yes, he had diabetes. He took pills for it."

"An overdose of insulin can kill, for sure. And it's unlikely to be detected even with an autopsy, especially in your husband's case. But I don't get why anyone would use the shoulder for an injection site. Unless…"

"Unless he was asleep and they sneaked up on him and used the first available place that wouldn't show."

Fern couldn't hold back any longer, bless her heart.

Dugan looked approving and I wished I'd thought of it first.

"Right you are. This carpet is thick. If they snuck up behind him, and I say they because one could have put that pillow over his face to keep him still and not make a mark on his body, while the other one slipped in the needle—Oh, I'm sorry." He reached to touch my arm.

I struggled to compose myself while absorbing all that might have happened to George and no one here to help him.

Fern took my hand and pulled me to the couch where she pushed me down gently.

"Sit."

I shook my head. "Later."

"Hang tight to those numbers. I have a colleague who is a cryptographer, and we might have to call on him.

"A what?" Fern asked.

"Someone who specializes in computer security. One example is, if a suspected criminal deletes everything on his hard drive, the police can still access it. Usually. Can I see the pajamas now?"

"I'll get them," Fern offered. She moved quickly to the laundry room off the kitchen where I had put them away in a small garment bag.

When she came back, he reached for the package and set it carefully down on the dining room table. "Great thinking not to throw them away or wash them," he commented, peering closely at the back of the PJs with his handy-dandy magnifier.

I didn't tell him right or left side, thinking it best that he discover the pin prick spot of blood if he could, on his own.

"Ah hah!" He held up the silky material. "Tiny, and I can see how all of them missed it. Even if they'd seen it, they might not have paid attention. Mosquitoes bite and leave tiny marks like this, or he might have scratched an itch. Since your doctor was here and made the death pronouncement, no one would have noticed." He held it up higher toward the chandelier. "It's a definite pin hole all right. Needle sized." He folded the top and placed it back in the bag. "Take care of this. We don't want to lose it."

I nodded. What would Junior think if he found out his father was murdered? The thought just came to me in a rush, and I felt nauseous all of a sudden.

"You do know that bringing this to a head could cause your husband to be exhumed? Not for sure. They wouldn't probably find anything new."

It was like he read my thoughts. Junior came to the funeral, but after giving me a couple of pats on the back and a hug or two, I could tell he wanted to grieve alone. He wouldn't appreciate coming here for a repeat. "Fern and I talked about stirring the pot so to speak. It would be hard to contemplate the idea of digging up poor George."

"Not only that, but you have so little to go on, with

George having no enemies to speak of and even if his gambling came to light, everyone knows a bookie wouldn't kill off a client unless he absolutely had to. I'm afraid the cops wouldn't take you seriously. You'd have to get some kind of court order to exhume him. If you could."

Comforting words. "Let's table the exhumation idea for a bit, shall we?" George wasn't going anywhere. I wanted cremation for him and that would have ended all thoughts of exhuming the body, but Junior wouldn't hear of it and purchased the gaudiest casket he could find. Maybe he felt guilty for his frustration at his father's inconsiderate, untimely demise.

Dugan moved toward the door and sat outside as if he needed a breath of fresh air. He picked up his iced tea glass. As he sipped, he seemed to be thinking and blessedly Fern kept still. Finally he spoke.

"You say he'd purchased alarms recently. And yet someone slipped inside quietly enough to surprise him. How do *you* account for that? And when you returned the door was unlocked."

I'd thought of that early on and was convinced I knew the answer. Would he buy the idea? Or just think I was out for revenge for the company not wanting to give me George's pension?

"I think, and this is just conjecture of course, that if someone murdered George, it had to be someone he knew or someone with the ability to enter our house. George might not have set the alarm, knowing I would be home in a few hours. Anyone where he worked would have access to his keys and could make copies. Or George even might have left the door unlocked for me. But I doubt that."

Fern spoke up. "Oh! Remember you told me George didn't like to carry his keys in his pocket all day? He probably had a key holder in his office same as the one he kept by the door."

I knew Fern couldn't stay quiet for too long at a time, but she spoke the truth, just what I'd been thinking too. "That's right. Someone at work could have taken his keys while he was in a board room meeting or whatever and made a copy."

And I knew who exactly might have done it. The faces of Jordan and Carroll were imposed forever in my memory, along with the image of sleeping angels who should have stayed awake.

"And these same people might know your schedule, if you go out to the library a certain night?"

"Exactly!" both Fern and I said at the same time.

"Well, ladies, let's see what I can dig up. I'll be back to check the computer. May have to take it to the office if it involves a lot of time."

"I'm glad you met me," Fern piped up.

I'd heard her say that a hundred times, and it never failed to amuse me how it always stumped people for a blink of an eye. He was no exception.

He smiled. "Me too." He took her outstretched hand and bent to brush an air kiss over it.

That gallant gesture said a lot for Jake Dugan in my book. I walked him to the driveway.

"I understand you may be in desperate straits financially," he said. His gaze took in the English rose garden with the obligatory vine covered gazebo, the manicured lawn and the house with columns like something out of *Gone With The Wind*. I knew he didn't believe I was so desperate. "But I'd advise against working for Levine. He's a good guy, helped me out when I needed it, but that job—it could be dangerous. And the bookies, I don't think they'll harm you, but they will keep trying to intimidate you unless we figure out a way to put a stop to it. Maybe Levine would have an answer to that. Anyway, I'm worried about you."

"Thank you. I appreciate your concern."

After he and Fern left, I took a look at the envelope Levine had given me. I'd almost forgotten it. It seemed a satisfactory amount for my first job ever, but I doubted it would pay much toward a PI, even though Dugan hadn't asked for an advance which I assumed all private investigators needed.

His concern, along with Fern's, went a long way right now—with bookies harassing me; the pompous corporate clones about to chew up and spit out George's last asset and, incidentally, might have murdered him; the bank looking over my shoulder, ready to pounce any minute; and who knew what other debts George had incurred? I didn't blame me for feeling self-pity, but I took a deep breath and straightened my shoulders. I needed revenge, or at the very least, justice.

Chapter 13

I separated Levine's letter-sized manila envelope from the pile of mail I'd left on the dining room table and sat down to read the contents. It didn't seem like a big deal. A woman had skipped out on paying off a check cashing loan and didn't answer her phone or the front door.

I took a cab to her house and asked him to wait while I knocked on the door. I could have driven our car, but I wasn't used to city traffic yet. I'd thought of trying Uber, which might have been cheaper, but there were too many mixed signals about that, and I wasn't trusting my luck lately.

"No one's home." A sharp voice came at me from nearby bushes. I walked over to look down at a kneeling woman putting a flower from a pot into the hole she'd dug.

"Thank you. Any idea where I might find Ms. Walker?"

The woman straightened her back and sighed. "Last I heard, she was in the rehab place over on Sixty-Second Street. She tripped on something a worker left out on the sidewalk and she's suing the city. But she busted her knee when she fell."

She said all that in one breath. Well, that seemed simple enough. I doubted Inez Walker could get away from me too easily if she was in therapy. All I had to do was deliver the subpoena and collect another fee from Levine.

"I appreciate the information. Thanks."

"Are you a friend of hers?"

"No, not really. I—we have some business to take care of."

"Good luck. She owes everyone in the county. She's a shopaholic, you know. She works somewhere part time, but when she's home she's glued to her TV and the programs where you buy stuff on QBC or some-such. UPS was driving up all hours of the day and night. Seems downright peaceful with her gone. Don't miss her for sure."

Again with the period-less sentences. "Thanks again," I said, backing away and heading for the cab parked at the curb.

I let the cab go at the rehabilitation hospital, sure that I'd be a while locating and talking to her. Once in the lobby, I signed my name on a sheet and, when the receptionist asked who I wanted to see, I asked for Ms. Inez

Walker. By her frown, I could tell this wasn't a good subject.

"She may be at lunch now. We don't like to disturb our patients then. If you go down the hall and to your left to room two-twenty-one, you can wait for her there if you like." She handed me a plastic enclosed tag to attach to my blouse.

Inez had a room all to herself, probably compliments of the city. I sat down in a chair close to the window and looked around. The room was utilitarian spare but clean and neat. The walls were painted a bilious green but the tiles on the floor were a more subtle beige. It had just barely turned twelve, so I suspected it would be some time before she came back. The pile of mail on her bedside table was too much to overlook. Even if I weren't serving a subpoena, I'd probably have been nosy enough to peek at it.

I shuffled through the bills, noting that her address was a post office box and all her mail had been forwarded. So her bill collectors didn't know where she was. Lucky for me, I'd caught the neighbor lady outside, because it didn't look like Ms. Walker would open her door to a stranger either.

All the while I rifled through the bills, I expected a nurse or Inez to catch me at it, so I hurriedly put them back on the table and sat down to look out the window. An hour passed. I must have dozed for a time. When my head jerked on my neck, I looked at the wall clock and another hour had slipped by. I got up and walked to the door, stopping an orderly passing by.

"Do you have any idea where Inez Walker might be? I thought she'd return to her room after lunch."

He looked at his schedule. "She probably went early to therapy. She's due for the whirlpool bath this afternoon. I'm going to take her back to her room in…" He looked at his watch. "…in ten minutes." He pointed around the corner. "I don't think she'd mind if you visited her there."

I walked in the direction he pointed and began to think he'd told me the way out. The hallway just kept going and going. It seemed as if patients able to do the whirlpool therapy were given a lot of privacy. I passed three semi-opened doors, all empty of inhabitants. The next door was closed and the sign said *Occupied*. The treatment order for Inez Walker was clipped to the door.

I knocked, at first tentatively, and then with my knuckles, harder. No one answered. I tried the door knob, and it turned so I pushed it slowly open. I didn't know what to expect. Did the patients take their baths nude? I didn't want to see any such spectacle. On the other hand, how could anyone refuse to sign for a subpoena in that condition? I got my pen and paper ready.

"Ms. Walker?" I saw a smallish figure, draped in a sheet, sitting upright in the bath. The bottom hem of the sheet was in the water.

She didn't answer, and I wondered if a person could

fall asleep in a bath. Why not, if it was warm and comfy? I'd just dozed off in a hard chair in her freezingly air conditioned room not minutes before.

"Inez Walker?" I moved forward slowly, not wanting to startle her. The room was small, and in two or three steps I was at her side. The shrouded form still didn't move. *Shrouded.* That word hit me in the stomach and I gasped. I reached over and took the top of the sheet gingerly between my thumb and finger and lifted. When it came off, I reached behind me to fall into a chair. Anyone could plainly see Inez Walker would never order anything again from QBC.

Now what should I do? How did she die? Peacefully it seemed, since she had a little smile on her face, and her eyes were closed as if in sleep. But I could tell from the color of her skin and the fact that her bony chest didn't move, she was a goner. The part of her in the water was shriveled and wrinkled, like she'd been there for some time. But I'd never heard of an abundance of wrinkles killing anyone.

Oh, lordy, I shouldn't be involved. I'd probably have to answer questions from the police. How would that look later when I brought up suspicions about George's demise? Dugan said family members were always the first suspects.

Fairly certain that she died of natural causes as the papers always say, I stood up, indecisive for a long moment. Then I got out a hanky from my purse and wiped off the chair where I'd touched it. I lifted the sheet and carefully draped it over her again. Now for the door knob, and I could try and slip out without being noticed. I had signed in, but I didn't write her name in the line for visitors. Maybe they'd forget. I'd only seen and spoken to two people.

I looked at Inez Walker one last time and hoped they'd find her soon. I didn't know how hot the water was but I hated the idea of her cooking in there. I closed my eyes and said a prayer for her and exited the room.

I saw an exit sign that I'd passed before and hoped it wouldn't sound an alarm when I opened it. So far so good, I pushed out into the fresh air and inhaled to get the scent of death from my nostrils. Belatedly I wondered how Levine would take it. Maybe I shouldn't tell him until I could attach an obit from the paper to her file.

I walked a couple of blocks before I called a taxi. Sitting back, watching traffic zooming by, butterflies began dancing around in my stomach and I didn't know how I'd done what I did and stayed so calm. I couldn't fall apart now, not until I got safely into my house and locked the door behind me.

Chapter 14

I finally decided not to tell Fern or Dugan of my cowardly actions. But Levine had to know so I could ask for another case. When I arrived at Levine's office, I saw the lock on Dugan's door. I'd have to catch him at a later time with some questions.

I didn't expect a greeting and didn't get one when I slid the envelope onto Levine's desk and waited. He was working with numbers but finally looked over his half-frame glasses, his caterpillar brows wriggling like live things.

"So?" He looked at the envelope but didn't reach for it.

"I'll need another case." I really squeezed that out between tight lips because I'd almost decided that even though he paid well, was it worth it?

"Crap! Just what I need, a no-show. I thought the Patterson case was a fluke and you couldn't cut it, sister.

What the hell happened? She say no?" His voice rose in a parody of what he probably considered womanly speech.

"It's a little more complicated than that. You see Ms. Inez Walker is…is deceased."

He glared at me as if I might be joking. Seeing that I wasn't, he leaned back in his chair and rubbed his bony fingers across his bald head. "I just got that paper two days before I gave it to you. What happened?"

No need to complicate things. I shrugged and raised my palms. "What generally happens? She's dead. Period."

He narrowed his already beady little eyes, and I wondered what was coming next. He changed the subject abruptly.

"I sent a check to the temp agency and they sent it back. Said you didn't work for them. What's that about?"

I took a little stack of papers from his desk to whoosh off the dust from a chair to sit. This might take a few minutes. "I'm actually not from any temp agency," I confessed. Before he could insert a wisecrack I hurried on. "My husband died recently under mysterious circumstances. I was here to check into hiring Mr. Dugan and saw your ad in the window. I've never worked before in my life, but until I can clear things up, my finances are up in the air. Everything is being repossessed. I did okay with Mr. Patterson, and I couldn't help it if Ms. Walker died, could I?"

He tented the tips of his fingers together much like

Dugan did, but it didn't come off nearly as charming. "Guess not. You still get paid. Since I don't have anyone else at the present, you can try it again, I suppose."

I assured him I'd try my best and took the envelope he shoved my way. When I passed Dugan's office, it was still closed, and I couldn't repress a sigh. Such a nice man and he seemed to know what he was doing. I just hoped he was quick. I didn't have much time left, with the bookies threatening me and losing George's retirement if I didn't get to the bottom of his death and the disappearance of all my assets before I knew where I was going to live. As Mr. Levine would say, "Oy vey."

cℑcℑ

Later that evening I heard my mail box at the side of the house clang open and shut. The mail lady had come and gone hours ago. I peeked through the vertical glass window on the side of the glass door, catching a glimpse of a retreating male figure. When I heard a car peel away outside the gate, I carefully opened the door and saw that the metal flap on the mailbox was half open. I could see something sticking out wrapped in what appeared to be brown paper. I ran back into the house and called Dugan. It didn't take long before he showed up. For some reason he'd brought a dog with him. The dog ran to the mail receptacle and began growling and pawing the floor.

"Edwina! Get out of the house! Now!" Dugan shouted and called the dog back. He pulled out his cell phone and dialed.

I didn't wait for an explanation but ran through the door and stood out by the hedge at what I hoped was a discreet distance. *From what?*

Before he'd finished dialing, Dugan and the dog hurried outside to stand near me. "Sorry if I was abrupt, but this dog has a knack for locating bombs. I borrowed him from a friend in Border Patrol. I suspected there might be a letter bomb in your mailbox. The cops should be here any minute."

Who would do such a thing? Well, that was a silly question. Most anyone lately might be a candidate, and they'd have to stand in line.

It seemed only minutes until the bomb squad rolled up on my circular driveway along with three police cars and an ambulance. One older policeman walked up to Dugan.

"We got here as soon as we could. They'll check it out." He gestured toward two men who wore shields on their faces and padded chest covering.

"Thanks, Harry. I knew I could count on you," Dugan said and turned to me. "Harry is an old friend of my father's when they were both beat cops. This is Mrs. Edwina Hartley."

"Glad to meet you, ma'am." Harry turned to Dugan, grinning, clearly anticipating some juicy information because of the bomb threat. "Working on a new case?"

Dugan shook his head. "No. We're...ah...friends."

Must be Dugan didn't want to talk about my problems. Okay with me.

The dog had been staring intently at the men surrounding the mail box until then. I noticed Dugan had a hand on his head as if to restrain him from moving in that direction.

Just then one of the bomb squad came out the front door carrying a sort of brief case affair but I could tell it was heavy. Probably lined with special metal.

"We're taking her mail. Can't tell now if anything's lethal." One of the men stopped to talk to them on his way to the armored van. He motioned for the ambulance to leave and all but one of the cop cars followed.

"We'll be in touch, Dugan. If something's up, we'll have questions for Mrs. Hartley. If the dog gave warning, I'll lay odds the letter bomb is there. Good to meet you, ma'am, see you around, Dugan." Harry walked away with the bomb squad.

After everyone cleared out, I began to realize what could have happened, and my legs turned to jelly. Dugan saw my problem and took my elbow to lead me to a patio chair.

"Are you leveling with me? If someone's desperate enough to send you a letter bomb, then you're way in above your head."

Treading water, the thought came to me. I glanced toward the swimming pool, glad that it had been drained.

What a morbid idea. "I think I know who might be behind almost all my problems, but until I can prove to my satisfaction, at least, that George didn't die of natural causes, I can't move forward. I blame it on the corporation where he worked. I'm positive of that."

"I asked you before, would you take a chance on ordering your husband exhumed?"

"The idea is abhorrent to me. George would spin in his grave, and George Junior maybe would never speak to me again. He's a carbon copy of his father and hates disorder and turmoil."

Dugan's raised eyebrow showed his skepticism. "Even if it were to prove his father was murdered?"

I nodded, unable to say more. I didn't want Junior to know about his father's gambling and debts. And I certainly didn't want my son poking his nose into my business and bossing me around.

It hadn't taken me long without George around to realize how comfortable and safe I'd become over the years, wrapped in his overpowering attention. I was determined not to ever allow that to happen to me again, no matter what I had to do on my own to live my life.

"Digging him up could turn out to be useless anyway. If whoever killed your husband knew about his diabetes and gave him an overdose of insulin, for example, it would only take a few hours for that to disappear from his blood and not leave a trace. The killer could have used an overdose of potassium too. That also disappears."

I couldn't stop the shiver that ran right down my spine and raised the hair on my arms. Poor harmless George, he didn't deserve any of this drama, and he sure didn't deserve to be dead. But it did solve one dilemma. I wouldn't have to displace George from his final resting place. And to think I almost had him cremated, but Junior couldn't stand that idea.

Dugan stood, towering over me, his slender frame leaning forward, and rested his hand on my shoulder. "Will you be okay? If that was really a letter bomb, the police will come by to talk to you, and Harry will let me know. But in the meantime, what if someone tries something else? I have a buddy who lives nearby. I'll get him to hang around at least for a few nights until the police get the results."

"That's not necessary. If it is a bomb, they will probably be waiting for results for a while." By the stubborn look in his expression I knew someone would be watching, at least for a while.

I watched him get into his elderly car and drive off, pushing away the lost feeling that caused. Should I have told him about the money Fern and I had found? Something told me to keep quiet. I had stashed it in a good place, I hoped, and wouldn't touch it until I figured out what George had in mind to do with it. The thought that it might be part of the $50,000 GG&W claimed George embezzled nagged at me, but I couldn't let myself go there.

I stood and looked out over his precious rose garden and said out loud. "George, if there really is anything like Karma out there, I hope you are aware of all you are putting me through. But I am sorry you are gone, and I really do miss you. I know we loved each other very much." I didn't get an answer, of course, but I thought the wind chimes tinkled a little with a soft sigh and there wasn't any wind.

The next night, I thought I heard something outside. I slept with the window open and jumped out of bed to look out. From the second story, I could see into the back yard all the way to the swimming pool. Something had caused the security lights to snap on, and then they turned off again. It was probably the man Dugan had sent to watch out for me. I wasn't about to get my robe and go downstairs. I checked the new lock Dugan had installed on my bedroom door again and tried to go back to sleep. Since it was nearly morning by then, I finally gave up and sat on the edge of the bed. It was time to see Levine again. Should I involve Fern? She'd been pestering me lately with her theories and wanting to join me. I decided against it. There seemed to be enough drama, with Levine's help so far, and I didn't need more with my dearest friend tagging along.

Chapter 15

It was only when I caught a taxi and told the driver the address, I noticed his grimace in the rear view mirror. That made me wonder belatedly why that smug half grin on Levine's face, when he pushed the brown envelope across the desk. I could have sworn I heard a chuckle as the door closed behind me

The papers sprawled on my lap, and I ruffled from first to last as the taxi careened through traffic. Oh my, it appeared to be quite a distance away, but I still had some money set aside for emergencies. What could be so hard about this case? Admittedly, I hadn't been in very many bars or taverns as they used to call them, in fact, none so far. But if I was to hand the paper to one of the patrons, that didn't seem like such a biggie. Having a cozy beer in a neighborhood tavern should put anyone in a good mood.

When the cab pulled up in front of the bar, I swal-

lowed with a dry throat. The building should be con-
demned and probably would have been if it weren't at the
very outskirts of town. It was completely made of wood,
against all fire codes, certainly, and the tar paper roof
sloped down almost to the ground on all edges but the
front. It had windows, but they were so fogged up with
years of smoke and dirt that I barely saw lights inside.

I asked the driver to wait. He didn't look too happy
about the idea, and I wasn't sure he would do it. Judging
from the dozens of motorcycles parked out front, it could
be a Harley convention. At least when I glanced at them
on my way inside, they were mostly of that brand.

Inside, I leaned against the wooden door and waited
a moment for my eyes to adjust to the gloom. From
where I stood, I could hear the click of pool balls striking
together. The smell in the large room made my eyes water and my nose dried up until I felt the little hairs inside
stiffen. A mixture of stale beer, in a background of Pine-
Sol failed to cover up the oddly sweet smell of smoke
that didn't have the same odor of cigarettes. I thought this
might be the last holdout of the non-smoking rule that
governed all the other establishments.

Patrons nearby turned to stare at me in blatant curiosity. Barmaids rushed around in various stages of what I
viewed as tacky scraps of clothing. Besides the barmaids,
the only women I saw looked almost like replicas of their
male counterparts, with black leathers and hair in pony
tails.

I took a deep breath, regretting it immediately and sauntered forward to the one empty space at the bar. I was glad I wore my highest wedgies rather than my usual flats, or I would have had to rest my chin on top of the bar.

"Young man," I called out to the bartender who seemed bent on ignoring me.

Finally, he sauntered over and took a swipe at the counter, coming perilously close to my nose. "Yes? Have you lost your way, perhaps?"

I could tell this pseudo English accent wasn't his normal way of speaking by the subdued guffaws nearby.

"No. I don't believe so. I'm looking for Mr. Elvin E. Kerry."

Word must have flown around the room for suddenly even the clacking of the balls stopped and all eyes turned to me.

"Elvin? Elvin Kerry?" He stared at the papers in my hand. "Jesus, lady, you gotta be kidding!" The bartender's mustache quivered and the brown of his eyeballs were surrounded by too much white.

"What do you mean?" I managed to stammer in the face of his horror.

"You're not a repo man…er, person…are you?"

I shook my head. "Why?"

"Geeze. Elvin ran over the last repo man with his motorcycle. Put him in traction in the hospital for weeks I heard."

I swallowed through a suddenly dry throat. Was being a process server anywhere near a repo man? Person?

Just then a short stubby man stood before me, a caricature from an old western novel. He wore a ten or fifteen gallon black cowboy hat and stood on boots that I recognized as having severe lifts inside. Still, he was only a little taller than me. The next thing I noticed was his tattoos. He had a large spider web across his neck going down into his western shirt and one small tear drop tattoo under his right eye.

"You asking for me, ma'am?"

Thank goodness, he was polite. Even if it could only be a veneer.

I held out my papers and a ball point pen toward him, hoping my hand didn't shake.

He stared at me for a long moment. The bar had blossomed into a dead silence and everyone in it including the waitresses watched us. Then he jerked his head toward the door.

"Outside. We can talk."

A collective sigh went up around the room. As if they all had been holding their breaths.

Did I want to venture outside with this man who everyone treated as a Mafia Don? I didn't imagine the cab was out there waiting and even so, at the first sign of a struggle the driver would be long gone.

Levine knew about this, for certain, and was probably waiting to see my body also in traction in the hospital.

He probably wouldn't have even visited me. For the first time, I wished I'd brought Fern. She might have seen enough talk shows to know what to do next.

☙☙☙

The door closed behind us, and Elvin E. Kerry took my elbow gingerly to pull me away toward the parking lot. Was he planning to run over me too like he had done to the repo man?

I pulled back, dragging my feet, but the little man was surprisingly strong for his size, and I couldn't budge him. Where was my can of mace when I needed it? At the bottom of my purse, of course.

When he seemed satisfied that no one in the bar could overhear, he let go of my arm and stared into my eyes, as if wondering if he could trust me.

"I'm not a repo person," I said. "I've brought papers from the collection agency, but I think they understand not to touch your motorcycle."

"You remind me a lot of my aunt Izzie, although—"He looked me up and down from my royal blue power suit to my raffia wedgies. "—she was a biker, and didn't dress like you, but all the same…"

"And?" I prodded.

"Well, I'm just saying that I feel like I can trust you. With my life—actually."

I waited, not sure where this conversation was going.

"I didn't exactly run over the repo man, it was an accident. But they believe what they want to." He jerked his head back to indicate the bar patrons. "I went to visit him in the hospital and took him candy and flowers," he admitted sheepishly.

"That was nice," I managed, still not sure where we were heading.

"He promised not to tell anyone I came to visit."

"But why…I mean they all seem very respectful of you." I didn't know how else to phrase it politely.

"Hey, Elvin, get your butt in here and finish the game," someone hollered out of the door but slammed it closed again as if he didn't want to be identified.

"You have a rather odd name," I said, trying to make him more comfortable.

"Yeah, there's a story about that. My mother was coming off a meth trip when she had me. She tried to tell them what to put on the birth certificate. She was in love with Elvis. You know, the Presley singer guy. But the recorder thought she said Elvin. It's been a hard name to fight down."

"I can imagine," I said, wondering how much his mother's meth ingestion figured in his personality. I'd always heard that meth babies often suffered personality disorders big time.

"Are you really from Texas?" I looked pointedly at his hat and boots.

"Sure as shootin' I am. Dallas."

"And the tattoos? Did you get them in prison?"

He looked down and dug one pointed boot toe into the ground as if to find a hole he might fit into. His fingers reached up to touch the tear drop shaped tattoo on his cheek below his eye. "This one's real. Hurt like bloody hell. Excuse me, cussin's a hard habit to break. In the pen, the cons burn the heel of a shoe and mix the soot from that with…well, might as well say it…urine…and inject it into the skin. They usually use a sharpened guitar string and attach it to an electric razor."

We both shuddered.

I noticed his knuckles, three round dots on the right hand. I pointed.

"That means time in the joint. Some guys have all their knuckles dotted."

I ventured closer and reached to touch his neck and the spider web racing down it, "You had that done? Not in prison, I hope."

"You kiddin' me? I ain't that foolish or brave. I done it with henna dye, and it won't come off, even if I'm caught in the rain. But I have to re do it every couple of months or it wears off."

"But why?" I remembered asking that question before and not getting an answer.

"That bunch of guys in there have been my only family. I got no one left back in Texas or anywhere else. Not since I was knee high to a…" He lifted his hands as if he ran out of words.

Actually, he wasn't knee high to much even now, but I kept my sarcasm to myself. He seemed so earnest, as if he needed me to understand. "I didn't actually go to the Texas pen, but I had a brother-in-law who worked in one as a guard. Anyway, these fellows care about me in their own way, and I respect that."

"Speaking of respect, how do you explain their awe for you? They treat you like a Mafia Don."

He grinned and took off his hat to slap against his thigh. "Aw, I think they call themselves Cosa Nostra now. Anyways, the first time I came to this place a couple of years back, it looked real interesting. I saw the guys talking and laughing, and they looked almost like a family. I won a lot of money on a lottery ticket, and I'd always wanted a bike. So I bought a Harley, got my tats, the real one and the others. And tried really hard to learn to ride the bike before I came here." He looked uneasily toward the door, as if afraid someone would come out for him. "To make a long story short, when I pulled up, I hit the gas instead of the brake and knocked over three big ones."

"Oh, my heavens. Did they want to kill you?"

He laughed. "You bet they did. They came pouring out of the place like an ant den had been stirred up, with murder in their eyes. I had to do some fast talking. I told them I was just out of the pen, had recovered my stash from the robbery, and decided when I pulled in here that I didn't like those three bikes."

"You mean you let them think you did it on purpose?"

He nodded. "I couldn't see any other way out. It was a huge bluff, but it was all the ante I had to put out on the table. When the three owners came and crowded around me, I can tell you I still feel it. But I couldn't show my hand. I began to peel out hundred dollar bills and said to the three, 'How about new bikes. I didn't cotton to them bikes, and bet you didn't like them so much neither.' Jake, the leader at that time said to me, 'Son, you gotta have the biggest balls in all of Texas.' Then I went for another big bluff. By that time, I figured it was all or nothing." His mouth turned down in a grimace. "I've been beat before on account of my size so I wasn't real scared, although I don't cotton much to pain."

"What did you do next?" His story fascinated me. Finally, someone who had more problems than I had.

"Some of them wore T shirts with HD in big letters on the front and back. I walked up to each one and poked a finger in their chests and said 'Hot Dog?' real loud."

I didn't get it, besides the finger poking of course.

When I must have looked puzzled, he grinned. "They frowned and said a few choice words, but I knew the initials stood for Harley Davidson and they knew I knew it too. After that, they all started pounding me on the back, telling me I had *cajones* bigger than three bikers put together and dragging me in for a drink."

His story was so preposterous, I had to believe him.

"Why didn't you pay off your motorcycle then?" I figured I'd better get back to the reason I was here. I didn't want to follow him back inside in case they came out for him.

He shrugged. "I wasn't sure I'd like a Harley. I saw this mother of a BMW and…but since the guys mostly all have Harleys, well…"

"So do you have enough money to pay it off? I'd like you to sign this if you will and let me get on with my job. You just have to show up and pay the late charges and everything will work out okay."

"And I won't have to run over you to show off to my buds?"

I was speechless for a moment, thinking he might be serious and then saw the crinkle lines at the side of his eyes.

"Do you have any extra copies in your reticule?" he asked.

Reticule? The word stopped me for a moment and then I nodded and pulled out a copy.

He reached for the papers. "Let's do it quick. I don't want to explain how I let an elderly lady get the best of me."

Elderly? I wanted to smack him. Fifty was the new forty now and so on. Didn't he know that? He was probably pushing thirty himself.

"Let me sign the paper then you call your cab back here on your cell." He scribbled his name on one of the papers and handed it to me, his back to the bar.

Puzzled, I called the cab, then before I could turn toward the street, he began striding back and forth in front of me.

He exploded with a fake rage so believable I was ready to run. He raged and stomped around, shouting until some of his buddies poured out of the building and stood watching. He tore the extra paper I'd given him and stomped them into the dust at his feet. It was quite a spectacular show. When the taxi pulled up—across the street at a safe distance, I noticed—Elvin winked at me, and I turned and ran as if my life depended on it. Shouts of laughter followed my hasty exit, which ate holes in my dignity. But I didn't mind. Elvin was back again.

I couldn't wait to plunk the paper on Levine's desk and watch his expression.

I wanted to get home, have a nice glass of wine, and sit for a while to let myself breathe. Then I would call Fern and tell her about my adventure.

Chapter 16

As soon as I arrived home and had my glass of wine, I went upstairs to shower but something made me pause on the stairs half way up. If I'd been a dog, I would have sniffed the air. It was charged with an unfamiliar essence. Living with George for so long and since we had always been the only ones to come upstairs, I sensed *intrusion*.

What should I do? Go back down and call someone? Who? My can of mace was downstairs tucked safely away in my purse on the dining room table. I glanced at the bottom edge of the stairs where George kept a baseball bat. Ostensibly this was for protection, but I could never see him wielding it with any strength. It was no longer in its rightful place.

My legs wobbly, I sat on the edge of the stair step a moment to collect my thoughts. Listening, I heard no noises. The house was silent as a tomb. Bad image.

Should I try to sneak down and retrieve the baseball bat? Too far to go for the mace in my purse.

I pulled a long straight pin with a pearl top out of my scarf and held it in front of me as I stepped upward. I wasn't being brave but I had no place to go. This was my home until they took it from me.

Opening my bedroom door cautiously, I peeked inside. Total chaos. The mattress was pulled from the bed frame and half on the floor, the bedside table drawer pulled open, hanging askew. I didn't take time to inventory. My first thought was someone hiding in the walk-in closets. I crept forward, pin in hand, and said a thank you prayer when I saw no one lurking inside. I had the creepy sensation of someone clutching my ankle from under the bed but I couldn't bring myself to look under there.

Making my way past strewn clothing on the carpet, I went out in the hallway to my hobby room. It was in worse shape—if that could have been imagined. No drawer was closed, no box upright or the contents neatly intact as I had left it. I sat down heavily in a nearby chair and held my head between my hands, a headache like I'd never believed zinging into my head. I pushed it back with sheer willpower. Now was not the time for one of my migraines. The only light in the tunnel was that I no longer sensed anyone's presence.

Whoever had done this was long gone. He or they must have watched me take a taxi and figured I'd be out a while. It had to be more than one person to do all this damage. What were they looking for? How did they get inside?

The money? Oh, lordy, could they know or suspect that George had brought home money? I closed my eyes and blessed my foresight as to where I'd finally decided to stash it. *Inside the hated giant heirloom chandelier.* George had hired a man to wire the monstrosity with a secret button to press under the table. When that happened the chandelier lowered slowly to settle like a giant ball of ice in the middle of the dining room table, and I was able to clean it myself without hiring a maid. True a maid came in once a month but that was all I would allow. The maid service was one of my birthday presents from George, if I remember correctly.

The chandelier had dozens of nooks and crannies within the glasswork. If one of the spaces was clear and let light shine through, the next space would be opaque from colored glass. I stashed the money there. Thank goodness. I thought of the papers I'd hidden beneath the carpet and ran back into the bedroom. They were undisturbed. Whoever had searched here was looking for bigger things than pieces of paper.

George's study. Surely they had checked that out. I went downstairs and looked inside the room. It was a mess, with papers strewn everywhere and file drawers gaping obscenely. I went to the computer. It looked as if someone had tried to get into it, but since George had installed a password, they wouldn't have had any luck.

He'd had a laptop somewhere but I didn't see it. They must have taken it. Chills sped up and down my arms. Would that make anything I tried to do worthless if they found some important information on the laptop? My only hope was with the password he'd likely put in, maybe they wouldn't get much. Or if George was being really careful, then he didn't put anything incriminating on it. Incriminating? I couldn't believe my mind was leaning in that direction. But what about all that cash he'd brought home?

I thought of my options. If I called Fern, she would demand I come to her house. If I called Dugan, he would probably insist I go to a hotel for the night. He had warned me about getting involved with the law until we had more to go on. Did he mean in an instance like this? Nothing had been stolen as far as I could tell. Wouldn't the police be curious as to what the intruders were looking for? Deciding that the perpetrator, as they called them on TV, would not have any reason to return, I checked all the doors again. Oddly they were all locked. I changed clothes and showered but the smell from the bar lingered in spite of my shower and washing my hair. When I called Fern, she said she'd be right over.

I sat by the door, reluctant to unlock it until she arrived. When I let her in, she slanted a look at me as if to ask why I locked the door, but then she bounded in with her usual enthusiasm.

"What's up, girlfriend?"

We hugged and then I beckoned for her to follow me into the study. Her mouth dropped open and for the first time in almost never, she was speechless.

"That's nothing. Follow me upstairs."

She stayed close behind me, almost running over my heels, and I showed her the bedroom. She trailed silently after me into my hobby room.

"Oh, my god! Did a tornado somehow get into your house?"

She was being facetious, but I knew she was waiting to collect her thoughts. And her questions.

"Did you call the police?"

"Not yet. Wouldn't they wonder why someone did this and what they were looking for? Dugan cautioned me to stay out of the limelight in case I became a suspect if it was true that George was murdered."

Her eyes got round, the whites surrounding the brown pupils. "*You* would be a suspect?"

I nodded. "That's what Dugan said. If I reported this and it somehow got into the papers, the wrong people might suspect that George *did* bring something home. I think this maybe just a case of bookies searching for easy money."

"*Just a case*? What if you'd been here? How did they get in? Are you sure you checked really good to make sure no one is still here hiding someplace?"

She spoke in one long sentence, not taking a breath in between. I actually saw goosebumps on her skinny arms. It was the first time I'd ever seen her so over-whelmed. "I don't know how they got in. I checked the doors and windows, and they're all locked. Of course no one is up here."

"Did you call Dugan if not the police?"

I shook my head. "I didn't call Dugan yet because he might suggest I go to a hotel for safety. I don't want to do that. Money-wise or just because." Fern knew better than offer her place. Neither of us wanted to involve her husband. He might have wanted to buy sheets of plywood and board up all my windows and doors. Besides, his dog, T Rex didn't like me.

Speaking of windows and doors…we went downstairs and without a word between us, we each began to examine all the windows and doors. Again.

It didn't take us long to figure out nothing had been jimmied or disturbed. The high widows that stretched nearly to the ceiling were all intact and there was only the patio and the front door. George had a company install burglar alarms all over the place but that was the first place I'd called to cancel the services. In retrospect, maybe that was a bit premature of me, but it was very expensive.

We went into the kitchen to make us a cup of coffee.

Someone had a key. That was the only explanation. I saw by the look of worry on Fern's face that she'd come to the same conclusion.

After I called Dugan, it didn't take him long to come

clear across town and knock on my door. I showed him the rooms and then we three sat down at the dining room table. I'd already made coffee for Fern and me so I poured another cup for Dugan.

"We didn't touch anything, because of possible finger prints, you know," Fern said. "Of course, criminals use plastic gloves that medical people use and that way they can feel objects better."

Dugan grinned at Fern. "For sure," he said. Then his eyes reflected concern. Was he assessing my vulnerability? At least I saw no pity there.

"Don't worry about me," I assured him, striving to keep the waver from my voice. "I don't stay with gloom for long. It's always been kind of like a wind that blows through my life and right out again. I'm fortunate that way, and George was a big comfort."

Fern rushed to give me a big hug.

"I'll check it out myself," Dugan said. "But you say no windows were broken? Are you sure you locked the doors?" At my nod, he looked toward the sliding glass door on the patio. "That would be a breeze getting into but…" He got up to check the door and came back to sit again. "Nope. Nothing out of order there."

I swallowed, unable to speak through a dry throat.

That didn't slow Fern down. "If someone has a key then we need to change the locks. She hasn't been evicted yet, and that may take a long time through the courts. She needs to be safe."

Dugan regarded her with a little twist to the side of his mouth, which I couldn't interpret.

"For sure," he finally said.

"That's it?" Fern wanted to know.

"Well, I'm thinking. I don't know if we should report this or not. But the complaint was filed about the letter bomb and—" He broke off when Fern interrupted him.

"Letter bomb?" Fern leaped to her feel, upsetting her coffee cup. She hastily wiped it off the shiny surface with the white linen napkin I'd provided.

Dugan turned to look at me. "Oh, you didn't tell her? I thought being as she's your best friend and seems to know you from babyhood, you'd have confided in her. I didn't mean to upset anyone."

"No, of course you didn't upset anyone," Fern said with frost covering her words. She glared at me. "When were you going to tell me?"

"Okay, I'm sorry. I was going to tell you about it, but I knew you'd get all bent out of shape. Dugan suspected something when he saw my mailbox cover askew and called in reinforcements. The dog found the bomb. No harm done."

"Then maybe it's time to tell him about—the money." She said the sentence and then silently mouthed the last two words.

Dugan sighed. "What about the money?"

"You read lips?" I asked, stalling for time to think.

"Certainly. That's part of my resume. I can read up-side down too."

"Come into the dining room. I'll show you." Both Fern and Dugan followed me.

I pushed the hidden buttons and the chandelier grad-ually descended, almost touching the table, but just hov-ering over the top. I reached inside the crystals and re-trieved the stacks of money, turning the big chandelier around as I went and putting the bills in neat little stacks on the table. I let the chandelier go back in place to make room, and nodded to Dugan to proceed. It was somehow gratifying to me that Dugan lost his Mr. Cool persona momentarily and his mouth opened in a big O.

He gingerly spread out the hundred dollar bills. "You know there could be fingerprints to be had on these?"

"We…uh…thought of that. But it didn't seem to matter." George's prints might have been all over it and then again, since the money looked brand new, maybe not.

He regarded the bills. "How much money? Is this all you found?"

"Since it is all in hundreds, we counted one hundred thousand dollars total."

He whistled. "My God, and right under your nose."

Resentment flared for his insinuation that George had hidden yet something else from me. Then I agreed. "How do you suppose I could know about this? When I didn't know about any of his other secrets?"

His eyes reflected my hurt and he grimaced. "Sorry. I didn't mean anything by that stupid remark." He picked up a pack of hundreds and took out his magnifying gizmo to look closer.

At my raised eyebrow, he smiled as if a little bit embarrassed. "A handy-dandy tool for us professional detectives," he said lightly. And then bent to look over every part of the top bill.

We waited. I was surprised that Fern held her tongue but knew she'd be drawn into the drama of the situation.

Finally, he looked up at us. "I think these could be marked bills. I don't find any outward signs of marking but there are newer ways to do it." When he saw that we expected more, he cleared his throat. "Don't suppose you'd have any more coffee. I could use another cup."

"For heaven's sake, what a hostess I am. Of course. Just hold that thought until I get back." I hurried into the kitchen and turned on the special coffee machine that George had to have. Expensive and made only one cup at a time. Hmmph.

When I brought out the tray for all of us with fresh coffee and set it down, he reached for a cup and sniffed. I could tell he was happy with it.

After he'd consumed half a cup, hot as it was, he touched the bills lightly. "First off, Edwina, don't be thinking your husband was in the process of tripping out on you. If he'd wanted to do that, he would have sent this money to a Swiss or Bahamas bank account."

He must have read the doubt that I couldn't keep from my eyes. I managed a weak smile.

"There are many new ways of marking paper money. For example, banks and FBI and other entities have access to microchips. It's very tiny, like the smallest grain of rice, and can be woven into the paper money. The ones I know about are only point-four millimeters and can store security codes for surveillance and ID tracking. I'm pretty sure our airport security has this technology to read in some of the larger airports."

Fern and I exchanged looks. Even *she* didn't know about this wrinkle.

"How do we find out? And how would George have come by such money?"

Dugan finished his coffee and sighed. "That's what we have to discover. First how and why he acquired this money. Was he blackmailing someone? That would make sense that person or persons would want him de—out of the picture."

"What if he was working for the police? Or the FBI?" Fern piped up.

"Exactly. We don't know any of these answers."

"I think the first place to begin searching is at his place of work," I said.

"You're right, and since you are concerned about his pension, much of that exploration will naturally have to be done by you. But with utmost caution. If George was murdered, they wouldn't think twice about killing you."

"Me? How could they hope to get away with two murders?"

"Maybe they could make it look like suicide. You were distraught over George's double life or you missed him so much you couldn't live without him."

"Oh, lordy, that makes too much sense, Edwina. You have to be careful." Fern was nearly wringing her hands in distress. I wanted to hug her.

"It needn't be so stressful as all that." Dugan touched his hand to my shoulder in comfort. "Someone knows the money is missing, and they must suspect George of taking it. So you would not be in serious danger until they find it. However, if they thought you knew anything..." He shook his head, a deep frown between his eyes.

George, what happened to you? Were you frightened and knowing someone watched you? Why couldn't you have confided in me? I could have at least been there for you. Maybe not enough to help, but standing at your side.

"I don't think the two men from George's work who came to my house would have any reason to suspect me of anything but being a clueless housewife who wasn't even aware of her husband's gambling." I tried to push away the rush of self-pity that threatened to overcome me. No, not in front of Dugan and Fern. I sucked it up and looked at them. "I can do what I have to do. Don't pity me, I'm learning," I warned them both.

Dugan gave me an accepting nod. "I don't think anyone is going to pity you. But, for now, you should stay away from George's workplace. They don't know me so I can pretend to need accounting help."

I doubted that would work for long when the subject of money came into play but I let it go. For now. The key might be in those papers under the rug. Dugan must have forgotten that I mentioned them. I wanted to be the one to clear George's name since even Fern had doubts about him and Dugan did too.

Chapter 17

As soon as Dugan and Fern departed, I locked the door behind them and hurried to get the papers under the carpet. When I held them in my hand, smoothing out the wrinkles carefully, they didn't make sense. I searched the closet in his office again and under a pile of papers, which I thought unusual since he never left piles of anything lying around, I found the computer. Whoever had ransacked the house hadn't seen it. Taking it back to the desk, I didn't see a charger, but I hoped I wouldn't need it. I didn't know how to begin. I looked around for a place to plug in the thumb drive and found it on one of the corners of the computer.

Did George use a password? That would finish this in a hurry unless I could come up with what he might use for one. Maybe I would eventually have to ask Dugan to dig up someone specializing in cryptography as he had suggested, but I had to admit to a certain amount of stubbornness. I didn't want strangers possibly turning up evidence of George using stolen money to stash away in banks. I'd rather find that out myself, but deep inside I still doubted he would have done this for his own gain. I'd finally come to grips with the idea that George had a hidden sickness, gambling. I wasn't forgiving him, at least for not telling me so we could work on it together, but I had enough faith left to not believe that he would embezzle.

When the screen lit up I was elated. But maybe too soon. I didn't know what else to do so I keyed in the first set of numbers. Nothing happened. I needed a password. I typed in my name, George Junior's name, the name of the gardener, everything I could think of, and then inspiration hit me and I typed in *When Angels Sleep.* Bingo!

Numbers flashed all over the screen, in a kaleidoscope of brilliant flashes of colors. I had to look away to un-bug my eyes. Was this what George referred to as a "dreaded virus?" I closed my eyes to the screen and doggedly typed in the next set of numbers from the papers which included two letters and ended with a capitalized M. The chaos on the screen diminished somewhat which gave me the incentive to finish typing in the other numbers. Every other one ended in the letter M.

The last line of numbers entered made the flashing die away and suddenly I was staring at a list. A mundane list of a grocery store, something named Leftovers and a pizza place. How odd was that? Each had its own address which I jotted down on a pad. I didn't know where George kept his printer. Weren't they usually attached to the computer? Had someone taken it? That would be odd.

At least I had a lead of where to go next. I'd visit the places on the list to see what that was all about. I decided it would be best to stay away from Levine for a while. Elvin was a hoot, but that business with Inez Watson left me feeling very dismal. I needed a Fern pick up I guess. When I called her, we decided to meet for lunch.

"I don't know what objects in our home George hadn't paid for, so it wouldn't be right for me to sell any-thing, would it?" Picking up a couple of French fries ab-sentmindedly, I put them down right away. I looked at my plate of burger and fries and her bowl of salad and the question of why she was stick-thin and I wasn't finally sank in after how many years of knowing her? The diet books claimed if you wanted to stay thin, observe how a thin person ate. Fern always ate the icing off of cakes and left the cake. Why was it I just recalled that now?

Losing George seemed to have many odd effects on me. I had become more observant of others, not relying on my husband to relay his thoughts about the person. During important elections, I'd usually voted the opposite of George but of course never admitted it to him. Now, I maybe would have told him, just to get a reaction. I real-ized I was changing, getting out on my own, like a tad-pole learning to swim. I'd even dug out my capris from the attic to be more comfortable around the house. Not to mention the two biggies—hiring a PI and going to work.

"It seems to me that you have some kind of investment in your belongings in that house," Fern said between bites of lettuce. "If you're sure you can't access your savings with Junior?"

I thought about it. Maybe I had been too hasty shutting out our son. He actually was a sweet, caring person, if a bit reserved. Should I have confided in him about the gambling, canceled insurance policies, and the embezzlement charge as well as my suspicion of murder?

The idea made the hamburger I ate want to rise back up in its original form. How could I even think of telling Junior all those sordid details? How would that help?

"George Junior could give me access to my money, I suppose. If I told him some kind of fuzzy story about why I needed it. Not that he would question me, of course, but, naturally, he would be curious."

"Naturally." Fern nodded, that little bobbed ponytail wobbling like a rabbit's butt. "Once you make up a convincing story about why you need the money and get that behind you, what's stopping you? Couldn't you use the money? What about Dugan? Are you making enough to pay him?"

When she made sense, it was amazing. I barely cleared enough so far with Levine to pay a deposit on Dugan, but so far he hadn't mentioned it. I didn't like the idea of being beholden to anyone, and that was bothering me. Even though Dugan hadn't done much so far. Well, actually he had, with the letter bomb and checking on the money. How could I have forgotten that?

"I'll get on the phone and call Junior when I get home. Meanwhile, I have a freezer full of food, and I'm sure the banks and credit companies will take months to get anywhere."

"I hope you're not forgetting the bookies? They aren't going to let up. Speaking of that, when I mentioned to Joe about the bookies—"

"You told your husband?' My voice rose several octaves and nearby people turned to stare.

"Well, of course, I tell Joe everything. Well, almost everything, on a need to know basis. Anyway, he knows of some bookies through a Mafia connection—"

"What? You're kidding. Joe is Connected? I know he's Italian but—"

"Italian/Irish," she corrected, not missing a beat. "As a fire fighter, he meets all kinds of people. It so happened a few years back, he and his crew did a good job of saving a very important Don's home and the man was so grateful he offered the guys boxes of illegal cigars and made them promise to call on him if they needed anything."

I thought I knew Joe almost as well as I knew Fern, but apparently not. He was a big, handsome galoot, towering over his wife. Didn't matter his size, she was the boss, but she'd always managed to keep that her secret.

"Joe has a temper. I never saw that, but you told me.

Only not with you. But I couldn't have him pummeling some unsuspecting bookie. I have enough problems without being accessory to mayhem and possibly murder."

"You really are being silly. Joe's like an apple pie. A bit crusty around the edges but sweet and juicy inside."

I didn't want to think about the juicy part so I tried to calm her down while I drove back to my house.

We went into each room and started picking up scattered contents and putting things back to normal. By now, I realized that Dugan definitely didn't want the police involved. While we were at it, I categorized some of the more expensive furniture and contents on a long yellow pad I found in George's office. The few paintings that I assumed were originals would have to wait to see if they were paid for, since he'd apparently maxed out his credit cards.

"What about the money? Did Dugan find out if it was marked?" Fern leaned over to pick up a jacket that belonged to George.

"Just hang it anywhere, don't be fussy." I almost felt his shiver of annoyance as if George stood next to me. "I haven't heard from him on the money yet." I decided to show Fern the list of businesses George had compiled from the secret numbers. Maybe she would know what it meant. I should tell Dugan too, next time I saw him. As soon as I showed her the list, right away she started jumping up and down. It made me dizzy, and I reached out to stop her on the down grade. "What are you doing?"

"I know what this is," she shouted. "George must have made a list of the corporation's money laundering activities. The crooks hide the illegal funds behind legitimate businesses."

"And you know this how?"

She grinned and shrugged. "Ah, you know, one of my TV shows I suspect. Maybe *Sixty Minutes.* Doesn't matter."

"I'd thought that might be the case and maybe I'd go to each of these places and sort of check them out."

Fern raised her eyebrow that went under her bangs, giving her an uneven look, almost making me laugh, but she looked so serious. "Might be an idea, but you'd need help. We could split the list."

"The pizza place and grocery store we might manage I suppose, but the junk yard?"

"Junk yard?" she echoed.

I managed not to look too smug. "I checked out the junk yard on the internet and, as unlikely as it may seem, it's called Leftovers."

"How odd. I would have imagined it to be an antique shop. But I'm relieved it didn't turn out to be a restaurant." She sighed. "We aren't likely to get much information unless we tried to get jobs with them."

I shook my head. "I've enough on my plate working for that tyrant Levine. Dugan may have some ideas. We could just frequent the places enough to get familiar with them and then maybe ask a few questions about who owns what."

"That would drag on forever. Show the list to Dugan and he can look them up on the internet maybe."

Well, for heaven's sake, so could I. I discovered George's password, and by now, I had made myself familiar with the darn machine so that it no longer scared me. I'd have to make up my mind where to start. We couldn't afford to be scattered.

Chapter 18

Days later, I was no farther ahead in finding out ownership and anything about the businesses. The junk yard was owned by an Italian man, but that seemed like profiling and politically incorrect to assume it was the first place to look.

I finally gave up and called Fern over to tell her my thoughts. We would begin with the junk yard.

She grinned, happy to get started on a project. "We can use my car. A 2014 Chevy Cavalier with a missing hubcap might get us inside and, between us, we could probably afford to buy a hubcap if they found one."

"You're missing a hubcap? How'd that happen?"

"That's just it. Joe can't know that I might replace it. On his way to Indiana for a hockey game, he lost the hubcap and, since his team won, he considers the lost hubcap a good luck charm. Silly man."

I grabbed my purse and we headed outside of town

to the junk yard, inappropriately called *Leftovers*. I could see that as a name for an antique store but a junk yard? As soon as we pulled inside the chain link fence, I noticed a large mastiff-looking dog chained nearby. He laid with his head on his paws and ignored us. He wasn't on duty, I suspected. We made it to the office without anyone accosting us, but once inside, I felt the walls crowding around me like a too-tight pullover sweater. All kinds of car parts hung from the ceiling and what seemed like a zillion hubcaps covered the walls. A tingle of apprehension sped up my backbone when I sniffed the air. I had a more-than-excellent sense of smell, often to my detriment, and I recognized a whiff of one of the corporate honchos. A coincidence? The pompous Jordan wore the same after shave or cologne. I'd smelled it as soon as he came inside my home. When the owner of the junk yard entered to greet us, I knew the scent hadn't come from him. He probably hadn't had a bath in a month of Saturdays. He was a large square man with a ten o'clock shadow, tattoos swarmed over his body, at least the visible parts. I swallowed past a dry throat.

"Well, hello there. What can I do for you little ladies?"

For once, Fern remained speechless, just when I needed her. "My friend here has an older car that's missing a hubcap, and there might be more…ah…things we could use."

He peered through the haze of cigarette smoke emanating from the side of his mouth. "Ladies aren't usually allowed to go into the junk yard. Insurance, you know."

"Oh, but I may need a side view mirror and the windshield washing gizmo leaks Maybe you'd have one of those."

The man yawned and scratched his stomach, plainly bored. "Nah, I don't want to look for all that with you two. If you walk careful like and don't go beyond where I can see you, I guess it will be all right. The Chevys are all over there." He pointed near the fence and thankfully away from the sleeping dog. "Name's Moody if you find something you need." He followed us outside, heading in the opposite direction.

I knew he had to carry liability insurance. He was just being suspicious for no reason that I could see. Unless he had something to hide, but from two housewives?

We watched while he strode away, back to the metal jungle where he appeared very much at home. "Stay close by the door and try to look interested in that nearby car," I told Fern. "I'm going back inside to check his desk."

"What if he has a helper?

"Did you see anyone else?"

"I guess not. I'll start a little whistling if I see anyone close."

I didn't even know she could whistle, but that should work. I went back inside and slid open a bottom drawer to start with. Since I didn't know what I was looking for, it wouldn't be easy, but I plowed through a lot of black greasy finger marked invoices and then shut that door and thought of under the desk drawer. I knelt down and peered under the long top drawer that held the pens, pencils, and blank statements. Way in the back corner I spied a taped on piece of paper that looked very suspicious. Before I could reach for it, a loud voice penetrated my concentration.

"Lookin' for something?"

Stunned for a moment, I raised my head too soon and hit the desk corner. I looked under my arm to see Fern standing with wide eyes and open mouth, nodding toward the front door, the one we never thought of Mr. Moody using.

I raised my head and rubbed where I'd bumped it. "I lost an earring and it rolled over this way." I bent down and hurried to unhook one from my ear and drop it.

"If it's valuable, I reckon I can use a metal detector."

He didn't sound as if that was a realistic idea, standing with his hands on his hips glaring at me.

"Here, let me help. Those are your favorites." Fern rushed over and knelt by me, gingerly patting the dirty floor carpet. She spied the earring I'd just thrown down while I continued to watch the junk yard man, not trusting him to do something drastic to us for annoying him.

We both stood, brushing off our knees and then our hands. She showed him the earring.

He didn't seem to look very interested but then turned and pointed to the hubcaps. "Got lots, but don't think I have one for a 2014 Chevy. If you want to leave your name and phone number, I can call if I find one."

The little hairs on the back of my neck prickled. That wasn't one of his normal offers. He didn't strike me as all that accommodating or polite.

"Thanks, but we'll come back another day," Fern said.

He shrugged and turned away, starting to sit behind the desk. Did he know about the paper under there? Maybe a scrap of invoice got stuck and torn off.

Once in the car, we made a U-turn on the lot and headed out on the dirt road. In my rear view mirror, I caught Mr. Moody staring at our receding car. Was he memorizing the license plate? Had I thrust Fern and her family into my problems?

She dropped me off at the house and went on her way. I hesitated to mention my fears about her involvement, knowing she would tell Joe. I called Dugan, but just got his answering service so didn't leave a message. Didn't want to go there and have Levine give me another assignment.

I closed and locked the door behind me, satisfied knowing the locks would be changed tomorrow. Dugan was sending someone over.

That little scrap of paper at the junk yard intrigued me. I couldn't let it go. It didn't look torn, but appeared to me to be put there on purpose.

But who and why?

Maybe it was time I paid another call to the accounting firm and stir up something there.

After showering, I changed into one of my power suits and took a cab to GG&W. In the downstairs lobby, I stood for a moment getting my bearings. The cold marble walls and floor left a decided chill to my bones, and I remembered the similar sensation of staring into Jordan's eyes. I marched up to the desk and confronted the young woman who looked up in question.

"I'd like to see Mr. Jordan or Mr. Carroll."

I expected her next words. "Do you have an appointment?"

"No, but I'm certain one of them will see me. It's in regards to my husband George Hartley's retirement benefits."

Her dinky shaved eyebrows lifted, but she picked up the phone to call. She waited a long moment and then put her hand over the receiver. "Both men are in a conference at this time."

I smiled. "Of course. I'll just sit over here and wait. I have plenty of time." I moved away to one of the plush chairs by the wall and pulled a paper back out of my purse.

She stared at me, spoke into the phone again, and said, "Mr. Jordan will see you in ten minutes, Mrs. Hartley."

It took twenty minutes, but finally, the elevator opened and Jordan made as if to step out. Seeing people surrounding me, he grimaced and beckoned me toward him. I never liked people doing that power thing, but I needed to be a little friendly to put him off his guard.

When I reached the elevator, he bowed me on. I waited a scant second until I saw someone coming our way to get on the elevator. We rode up together in silence. The doors swished open, and he led me into a large room, not a soul within. I swallowed. Surely if he was involved in killing George, he wouldn't dare harm me here.

He motioned me to a seat in front of a gigantic desk, another power maneuver. I sat primly, my hands folded over my purse, waiting to let him have a go first. I could tell by his frown and the straight line of his lips that my visit didn't sit well with him.

"The receptionist said you came in question to George's retirement. I thought we'd settled that matter effectively. As long as he...ah...misappropriated funds, we cannot in good faith provide retirement benefits. That will have to go to repay the missing revenue."

"I'm meeting with my attorney shortly. You've never shown me proof of your outrageous claim." I treaded on slippery ground here, thinking of the stack of money George hid in the house. But that was way over the $50,000 GG&W claimed he stole from them. Something was rotten for sure. Did George take the money from the firm? And if he did, why weren't they admitting it instead of saying he took $50,000?

He folded his long, pale fingers together at the tips, elbows resting on the desk, and peered at me as if I was such an insignificant specimen of humanity that he barely wanted to speak to me.

I held my anger in check and tried to manage only an appearance of annoyance while I waited for him to speak again.

He assembled his features into a semi pleasant look and his next words shocked me to the core. "I am pleased to understand you have found a little job to keep you busy I imagine. Are you out and about with your friend recently?"

His tone was soft but a hidden quality of menace lay underneath. What did he know? The only place I went with Fern lately was the junk yard. That could mean there was a connection, but did he believe me intelligent enough to piece that together? I didn't think so, he was testing me.

I managed to keep my voice level and glared at him. "Why is it you feel a need to check on my personal asso-ciations—where I go and who I am with? As if that is any of your business or the company's."

He shrugged. "I explained that it would be preferable all the way around if there is no notoriety attached to George's theft. Since you threatened us with an attorney before, we tend to keep track of certain people, just to insure our interests are not at risk."

"Not a good enough explanation. And then what would you do about it?"

His smile didn't reach his eyes. "There isn't much we would do or could do officially, of course. We just wish to stay informed."

"Did you snoop on all your employees? If you make a habit of that, you should have discovered George's alleged theft before—" I wanted to say before you killed him, but I didn't dare go that far. I'd already antagonized him enough that he might do something stupid that Dugan and I could hang something on.

He stood and motioned toward the door. "I believe this interview is at an end. I assure you if your threat of attorney occurs, you will be the loser, financially and in all ways."

"You may presume the interview is at an end, but it could turn out to be the end of you. I don't give up. My husband did not embezzle, and I intend to prove it."

I turned to leave, knowing that I'd poked a rattlesnake and not sure of where to go next.

Chapter 19

I became frustrated at what I saw as my lack of progress in clearing George's name and finding his killer, if indeed he was murdered. I didn't even have the certainty of that. It was as they say on TV, circumstantial evidence and a gut feeling that wouldn't go away. Plus the money stashed in the chandelier that had to have some kind of explanation.

It was time to see Levine again, although I dreaded it. He seemed to take a snide satisfaction in sending me on jobs that might put me in the hospital if not lying next to George.

Dugan was out to lunch, according to the sign on his door, when I entered Levine's office. In spite of what I considered darn good work, he didn't look pleased to see me. Was he ever pleased at anything?

"You're back."

I smiled and nodded. "Yep. Just dying for another

file." That might be the appropriate words to use for his choice of cases.

He pulled out a roster of names and ran his gnarled finger down the list.

"May I see that? I might want to choose my own file, since the last three were real doozies."

He managed a snort of what I assumed was a mini laugh and shoved it over to me. I still didn't want to sit on a chair in front of his desk, even though he'd finally removed the pizza box so I stood and looked over the names. None seemed any more promising than the next one until I reached the name Moody. I held my finger there and turned the paper around so he could see.

"What's that one about?" I asked.

"You don't want to go there. It's just a minor case of alimony back payment."

"Don't you think it's about time you gave me a break with an easy case?"

He tilted back in his chair until I feared he would topple over. "I gotta admit, you did pretty good for a novice. I am surprised. But this guy—I don't know much about him."

There could be many Moodys in the city. It wasn't an unusual name, but when I met the man at the junk yard, I had presumed that was his first name. I doubted there was any connection, but it seemed like a regular file with hopefully no problems. At least this time I didn't let Levine choose for me.

I never had involved Fern in my work, although in retrospect, I imagined she would have enjoyed it, with the exception of poor Inez Walker. I decided to wait until after six p.m., thinking this Moody person might work and not be home during the day. I changed into something a little less threatening than my suit and, when the time came, took the car out of the garage, and drove to my destination.

Mr. Moody lived in a rundown trailer park at the edge of town. When I drove into the park, I skirted around kid's toys in the narrow lane while dogs on chains in yards barked at me. I looked down to check the number and drove around toward the back of the park. Good thing I wore flats because the gravel around Mr. Moody's house was uneven and hard to walk on.

I crunched up the path, trying not to make too much noise. The subject wasn't supposed to want the subpoena, and I didn't want him running out the back door. I stepped up on the rickety porch, thankful no dogs lived here, or it would probably have been chained to that nearby cottonwood tree. When I knocked, I heard a loud TV that someone just shut off. I waited, paper and pen in hand.

When the door swung open, I know my mouth dropped as did his, and I came face to face with *the* Mr. Moody from the junk yard. Suddenly, I felt very alone. I shoved the paper toward him.

"I need your signature, Mr. Moody. Your wife filed

papers saying you are late with your alimony payments."

"Ex-wife. Come on in." He stepped back a pace as if he wanted me to squeeze by him.

Uh, uh. I didn't think so. He wore a sleeveless T-shirt with all his tattoos showing in brilliant colors and his jeans were unbuttoned at the waist as if he'd been sitting sprawled in a chair. He belched and I almost gagged on the stench of stale beer when he didn't bother to cover his mouth.

"Ain't you one of them broads what came out to the junk yard other day?" His beady little eyes reeked suspicion.

"Well, yes. But that has nothing to do with my being here serving papers. This is just a coincidence." Why would he care if he met me twice? I looked around to see the nearest trailer house quite close, and I heard people inside talking. I should be safe and might learn something from a visit with him.

I motioned him gently aside and walked into the room. I cringed when he closed the door behind me but pretended not to notice. He motioned to a couch facing the chair he'd obviously been occupying.

"I don't want to interrupt your television program," I started to say.

He brushed it off with a shrug and sat in his chair, watching me. Finally, he spoke, holding up his can of beer he retrieved from the end table. "Want a brewski?"

I shook my head. "No thanks. I just need you to sign

the subpoena, and I'll leave." I doubted I'd get any information from him and maybe he'd refuse to sign the subpoena, but I hated to go back to hear Levine's "I told you so." The fact that the junk yard showed up on George's notes and the scent of what I believed to be Jordan's after shave in the office kept me focused.

"I thought maybe you were the owner of the junk yard," I said.

He sneered, lip curling. "You mean *Leftovers?* What changed your mind? Maybe I *am* the owner."

I tried not to look around the shabby room too obviously, but I must have done so because he actually chuckled, the odd sound making me jerk around to stare at him.

"Nah, I don't claim to own it. A real money maker, junk yards, but takes money to make money I always say."

"Someone had money to start it then." I left the statement as a semi question.

For a moment I thought he wouldn't answer but he apparently felt in an expansive mood and likely didn't have a lot of visitors.

"A corporation owns it, I guess from another state, but I ain't for certain. Don't matter to me as long as I get my paycheck every week." He waved what I assumed was a check in the air and plopped it back down near his beer, but careful not to get it wet.

"Well, if you were the least interested, you could look at the name and address on your paycheck, I'd imagine." No use trying for subtlety with him, I reasoned.

He took a deep swig of beer and burped, rubbing his flat stomach. He could have been an ex wrestler or boxer, he had that sort of used up look.

"Don't care. This highfalutin' corporation bought out the former owner almost a year ago. That's when I saw the help wanted ad and signed on for the job. I don't have any complaints."

"Did you ask me if I wanted a beer? I could use one right about now, my throat's pretty dry."

As soon as he got to his feet and went out to the kitchen, I hurried over to the end table to peek at the check. I'd no more than picked it up and his voice sounded as if he was moving toward me.

"Wanna glass?"

"No thanks," I said and dropped the check just before he entered the front room. No time to read anything but that it was from a city in California. Chances were the name and address would not be a reflection of GG&W, since they appeared to be experts at money laundering.

I accepted the beer, not really wanting it, and lifted the can as a salute which he answered in kind. "So how long have you worked at the junk—at *Leftovers*? And by the way, that's an odd name for a junk yard, don't you think?"

He grinned, showing a big gap between his two front teeth. "Yeah, I figured it was kinda sissy, if you know what I mean, but, hey, the owners are from California, what do you expect?"

That meant he did know where his check came from. By now, I began to put two and two together and cursed myself heartily for not being more aware at the time. It had been about a year ago when George started closing the door on his study, not allowing my presence in the room. He'd never refused me the first thing in all our married life, now that I recalled. Had he figured out something was rotten in GG&W and was that when he started bringing cash home?

Moody was talking and I missed half of it with my wayward thoughts. I covered my inattention by taking another sip of beer and nodding as if I'd been listening all the while.

He reached forward for the papers in my lap and I tried to stifle the sigh of relief when I handed him the pen and documents.

"You know, the old lady is making more than me working at the diner, but hell, she don't report much of what she takes in with her tips so I have to pick up the slack. Ain't fair. Anyways, I'm glad to be shut of her." He signed and initialed it all and left the date for me to fill out, which was ok.

When he turned toward the TV, I stood and put out my hand to shake his. "Thank you, Mr. Moody, for making my job easier. As it goes, it's not always rewarding to bother people."

"Yeah, bummer job, I'd say."

He didn't get up to see me to the door so I gave him

one last little wave and walked down the steps and out to my car. I was anxious to get home and jot all my impressions on that yellow legal tablet I'd been using. Before I forgot even one little item which could be a clue.

Chapter 20

I awoke with a crushing feeling like my old hot flashes had come back. Suffocating heat crawled over me
without the relief of cooling perspiration. Then I realized the problem was not inside me but outside.

Someone had entered the house.

We hadn't changed the locks yet, was my first
thought. It was supposed to happen today. I leaped out of
bed, tangled in the sheet, and fell to the floor before I
could reach the bedroom door to check it. I didn't remember locking the bedroom door.

Before I could untangle my legs I felt hard hands
grabbing my arms and holding them behind me as they
pulled me to my feet. Fear made my legs tremble and
dried out my mouth so that I couldn't scream if I had
wanted to. Rough hands wrapped a blindfold around my
eyes, and it didn't seem to take a minute before my hands
were tied in front of me. Callused fingers moved against

my neck and pressed, and everything turned black.

I came to and pushed myself up in a panic, my hands tied and numb. My throat was sore, I must have been screaming. At one time, someone had stuffed an oily smelling rag in my mouth and I managed to spit it out. Darkness shrouded me, there was no light anywhere. How long had they kept me here and where? I rolled off the thin pallet under me and pushed with my knees to rise. I'd never been good at that maneuver but fear made it surprisingly easy to stand, although I was wobbly as a new born colt. I felt around with my tied hands in front of me and touched only air but kept moving straight ahead, finally bumping into a wall. I reached out my fingers and it felt like metal. Leaning against the wall, I raised my hands and worked off my blindfold. Didn't matter, it was still stygian dark. They'd kidnapped me from my bed-room. I still wore my new flannel pajamas I'd bought since I slept alone.

I knew where I was then. Ripples of fear coursed over me, and the goose bumps on my arms made the pa-jamas feel good. The smells of gasoline, stale oil, and the lingering smell of cigarette smoke told me I must be at the junk yard. What had happened to bring me here? Moody and the corporation creeps must have met and compared notes. Fern would soon realize that I wasn't home and that I'd never leave overnight without telling her. Surely she would contact Dugan, but how would they figure out where I was? And even if they came here looking, I remembered seeing at least a half dozen metal storage sheds and large containers inside the yard. Would they contact the police? They wouldn't be any better at finding me.

It felt easier to stand even though I had to lean on the wall to keep my balance in the dark. It was hard to tell how long I stood there, wondering how to get myself out of this mess when I heard crunching of gravel. Someone was coming.

A door grated open at the other end of the building, unfortunately away from where I stood. It was still dark outside. I saw that beyond the person at the door. A strong beam of flashlight struck me full in the face, blinding me.

"Ah. You're up. Boss wants you to eat and drink. Be ready for questions."

I didn't recognize the voice but it seemed muffled as if the person tried to disguise the sound.

"How can I eat or drink, I can't see anything and my hands are tied." I was proud of how my voice stayed firm even though I wanted to scream at this person.

He bent and rolled something toward me. It looked like a small flashlight.

"You took off the blindfold, but it won't matter in the long run."

If that didn't put terror in my soul, nothing would have. In other words, after they questioned me for whatever purpose, I would have to die.

He set a metal dish with a plastic fork and a canteen that might hold water. I waited until he left to figure out where the flashlight had landed. Cautiously, I stepped across the floor to where I thought he'd thrown it and bent down to feel around best I could do with hands tied. After a few hard bumps against what had to be pieces of metal, maybe car parts, I took a little more time to feel and finally grasped the small light with my fingers. It wasn't any larger than my hand, but I was thankful for some light. Batteries must be small, wouldn't last long.

I flashed it around the room and sure enough, parts of cars swallowed up half the room, looking like shadowed animals in the near dark. I walked toward the door and looked down at the meal they'd brought me. Some kind of a sandwich, unwrapped and already drying out, the crust curling at the edges. I picked up the canteen and imagined the soothing water going down my throat. Did I dare touch any of it? What if it was drugged or poisoned even? I moved back to the pallet and managed to sit down, not easy with hands tied. If I ever got out of this alive, I promised to join a gym. I'd had no idea how out of shape I was.

I couldn't prop myself up against the wall. The metal would be too hot in the day and cold after the sun set so I lay back down and closed my eyes, trying to give Fern mental telepathy, which for some odd reason struck me as funny. I must have dozed because when I opened my eyes again and sat up, the crack under the door showed light, and above me almost twelve feet I figured, a small dirty window showed light also. Unfortunately that didn't provide any illumination to speak of inside the room.

It felt like hours waiting and not knowing who would come to question me. I shined the light around and found an old beat-up metal footlocker in a corner. If I could reach that window, I could at least get some fresh air, although the window looked about Fern-size and I felt sure I could never shimmy out of it. I was thankful the locker seemed empty as I tugged and pulled it until my fingers had grown numb, but I could tell I'd scraped off pieces of skin on the fingertips. It seemed hours before I had dragged it under the window. I didn't know if someone would come again, or if they would wait until dark. With the dirt floor underneath, at least I hadn't made much noise.

Now that I had the footlocker in place, I needed to get it on edge since the window was still too high. I struggled to turn the footlocker but finally shoved the side against the wall. I found a piece of old dented car fender that I managed to drag and haul over and held the flashlight between my teeth so I could see what I was doing. I knew the fender was old—it was metal and not plastic or fiberglass. I pulled up the fender and stepped gingerly on it. It rocked like a ship at sail. Swallowing my fear of falling, I stood on tip toes and hoisted myself onto the narrow edge of the footlocker, fighting against the sudden tilting by leaning against the wall. I reached

up with my fingers to hold on to the window frame. If I
fell from here on the hard dirt floor, I would surely break
something. I swept away the insidious thought that it
might not matter what I broke. Sweat poured down my
face, and I tried to wipe it away from my eyes with my
shoulder.

When I had steadied the swaying somewhat, I felt
around the edge of the window and my fingers struck the
lock in the middle at the bottom. I pushed and prodded,
but it wouldn't budge. I moved my fingers around the
bottom and my heart sank to my toes when I realized that
the window had been sealed with old paint that was no
longer the least bit pliable. If I'd have thought to look for
an object I could have broken the window with, that
would have been a dream, but then I couldn't have
scrambled up the locker holding anything. Pajamas were
not known for having pockets.

The need to scream or curse washed over me, but I
did none of that, knowing I'd need all my energy to get
back down off the locker without killing myself. It was a
long jump, but I had no choice. Stepping onto the rocky
car fender would be no help. Not daring to wait any longer, I leaped off the locker, kicking back to keep it from
falling on me. Putting my shoulder down, I rolled into a
ball like I'd seen stunt men do in movies.

I cried out; landing on my shoulder was beyond any
pain I'd ever felt in my life. I laid still a few minutes to
try and collect my tortured body and see if I had any

moving parts left. When I rolled over and sat up, I ached in places that should have belonged to two more people.

By rolling to my knees and pressing my palms to the earth, I managed to stand. The falling locker and fender had made a lot of noise. Even so, they had probably stashed me in the farthest shed on the lot and maybe no one heard a thing.

The day dragged by and the metal shed heated up. I had pulled the pallet across the shed to be close to the door. I found an empty oil can and used that to relieve myself but if I didn't get a drink, I soon would have no use for it, I would be dried up. I picked up the canteen. I had to open it with my teeth, my fingers were scratched and numb. When I smelled the contents, I couldn't detect anything but chlorinated water which was normal. I heard an odd snuffling sound under the door and realized the big dog had come to investigate. I went to the door and ripped off some of the sandwich, sticking it gingerly underneath. It disappeared in a second. He did look sadly underfed when I first saw him.

I took a cautious swig of the canteen, letting the cool moisture sift down my throat. I didn't take too much since I hadn't planned to eat that dried up sandwich. The crazy idea that I might lose some weight threaded through my thoughts, and I couldn't believe that idea had entered my mind, considering my circumstances.

By now, my pajamas began to smell a little, and I knew they had to be dirty from rolling on the dirt and scraping against the rusty locker. I tried to keep from feeling how hot this shed could really get if it were summer. Thank goodness fall came a little cooler. This was so beyond anything I'd ever had to endure in my lifetime, and it came to me in a rush how very lucky I had been. It all fell apart when George died. Anguish for George and hatred for Jordan or whoever had killed him because of their greed flooded my mind and I wanted to smash something—someone. Not being a violent person, it surprised me that I could easily shoot whoever stood in front of me if I had a pistol.

Chapter 21

When I chanced to look toward the offending window, I saw either clouds or the beginning of nightfall. Underneath the door looked dark too.

In rummaging around, I discovered a pile of old newspapers. Good, I could read to pass the time. I dragged the pallet over to the narrow window and settled down as comfortably as I could manage. It was then I discovered the news print was too blurry to read. Only the headlines. I didn't have my reading glasses. The day seemed to grow darker.

I didn't have much longer to wait before I heard the crunching again of approaching steps. I'd thought a while back to stand near the door and plow my head into the midsection of whoever opened it, but my battered body simply refused to move from the pallet I sat on.

"You ate finally," he pointed to the tray.

I closed my eyes at the sound of Moody's voice echoing in my head. Was it the right thing to do to let him know I recognized him? Caution overcame my need to lash out. I'd best wait.

He aimed his flashlight in my direction, striking me in the face like a blow. I raised my arms to shield my eyes.

"You think we're gonna poison you?" he asked, moving the tray aside with his shoe.

"Maybe." I didn't want to mention drugs in case they might not have thought of that.

He snorted and I got a whiff of cigarettes and stale beer that must have bled out of his pores.

"You are in big trouble, moron. Mr. Levine knows where you live. Did you forget that?"

He snickered. "Won't matter. No one will ever know where you disappeared to." He moved as if to let someone else in, someone carrying a lantern. Moody stepped outside closing the door.

"Well, well, Mrs. Hartley. I hope you have been comfortable."

"Jordan," I snarled, wanting to hurt him badly.

He laughed and set the lantern down near the door, but it still shone across the room, lighting my corner.

I couldn't help but notice that even though I was tied, he held what looked like a gun with an extra-long barrel that could have been a silencer. He didn't come closer. Coward.

"I don't have the time or inclination to dally with you. Where is the money George stole?"

"How come you're doing your own dirty work? I would have thought you'd hire thugs to talk to me."

He smirked. "Doesn't really matter. I can't trust anyone to know the whereabouts of the one hundred fifty thousand dollars except myself."

I tried to keep the surprise from my eyes. We'd only found $100,000 that George had brought home. Was there more hidden somewhere in the house? Maybe George had spent some. No, I wasn't going to go there.

"I don't know anything about any money. Do you suppose I would let my home and everything I owned go back to the bank if I found money?"

"We searched the house and didn't find anything, but you came to the office. I would have never left you alone but I believe you found something. The location of the money perhaps."

I shook my head in denial. "I just came to pick up George's things. What was there to find? What are you mixed up with anyway?"

His inhaled breath let me know that I'd said something wrong. I was trying so hard to be careful, but my body ached in every part including the hair on my head and damn it, I *was* hungry.

He moved toward me, his slow steps menacing. The gun pointed at my chest made goose bumps climb over my bruised skin. He held Moody's flashlight and kept it shining into my face, blinding me.

"You'll never get away with this. Someone will come looking for me."

"It'll be too late, unless you tell me what I want to know."

"Where did this money come from? Why is it in stacks of cash?" I could have bit my tongue, the only thing in my body not hurting.

"Ah. So you *do* know about the stacks. I guess it wouldn't hurt to tell you. The money belongs to the Mafia. I held it back, hoping they wouldn't notice a measly couple of hundred thousand missing from the billions we helped launder for them."

Now I knew my goose was cooked for sure. He wouldn't be admitting this if he planned to let me loose ever.

"What makes you think George took the money?"

He waved the gun around to make a point, and I couldn't help flinching, since he didn't seem the type to be too familiar handling such a weapon.

"I suspected dear old George was working with the feds. Not sure about that, he could have just needed money to support his gambling. But he took the money and I need it back."

"Why don't you just shoot me and get it over with? I don't know where the money is. And frankly, if I did I wouldn't tell you." I wanted him to admit he had George killed but if I accused him, there wasn't a chance in hell I'd get out of here alive. Not any kind of an option anyway, but where there's life, there's always hope.

Jordan came closer, and I was sure he was going to strike me with the gun or the flashlight. I held up my hands in front of my face and he laughed. The bastard laughed. Without another thought, I raised to my knees and flung myself at his legs, trying to hit him anywhere I could with my tied hands.

He fell backward and rolled out of my reach. The flashlight spun away and he reached out to retrieve it but held on to the gun.

"That'll cost you, bitch," he snarled, leaping to his feet, and pointing the gun at me.

I managed to stand and face him. "If you're going to kill me, I want to be standing, looking into your eyes."

He backed away toward the door. "We'll see about that. I'm not much for torturing women but if you can live without food or water for a few days with the heat bearing down on this metal building, you'll tell me everything I want to know."

"And then what? You can't let me live, can you? What about Moody? You said you didn't trust anyone to do your dirty work and yet he helps you."

He opened the door and looked outside. "Moody's days are numbered. He knows too much. But you, I could let you go. When I get the money, if I framed George with our accusation of embezzlement upping the ante to a hundred thousand, that should silence you. And let me off the hook with the Mafia. I doubt you'd want his name slandered, and our attorneys could do a good job of it. I might just let you live." He laughed and slammed the door. I heard the lock snap and his footsteps crunching away.

I harbored no doubts that he was not going to let me live.

The dog came back later when it was total darkness outside, and I fed him the last of the scraps I'd been doling out each night.

Early next morning, the sun torched down on the roof of the building and inside felt blistering. I tried to imagine myself lying on a beach somewhere in the Caribbean, getting a nice tan. It didn't work. I walked to the tray Jordan had kicked aside and picked up the canteen. The cover had come off, I hadn't tightened it good enough with my teeth, and found only a few drops to wet my tongue.

I sat quietly on the pallet, not wanting to add any body heat. I'd been here three days and four nights, surely Fern and Dugan would have been searching for me by now. Toward evening, when the light under the door wavered with the setting sun and the window lost its bright light, Moody opened the door. He didn't come close, Jordan must have warned him.

"Ready to talk to the boss yet? You must be awful thirsty." He left the door partially open and I inhaled the fresh air along with a little respite from the heat. Unlike Jordan, he didn't come with a gun or a flashlight.

"You do know that when I die, you go too. He doesn't trust anyone with his secrets."

For a brief second, I saw what could be construed as pity in Moody's eyes and then he scoffed at the notion. "Not likely. I got too much on him to be afraid."

"You mean you've hidden evidence against him somewhere? That won't matter if you're dead."

"But he knows it and don't know where I hid it. He can't take a chance."

"I think you're wrong, Moody. He as much as admitted to me that you are expendable as soon as I tell him what I know. Which is absolutely nothing, for godsakes. When will any of you listen to me?" I almost believed myself, I tried so hard to be convincing.

"Naw, he's going to get me a good job in his corporation, he promised. And whether or not you know where that money is, you don't stand a chance in hell of surviving."

"But people will come looking for me. Mr. Levine has your name as the last person I took a subpoena to." I looked into his dark eyes and saw my death mirrored. No one would put two and two together in time to save me.

"How will they get rid of me? Can you at least tell me that?"

He kicked at the dirt floor with the toe of his shoe, taking his time to answer.

My heart thudded into my ears. I had a hard time breathing.

"I suppose you might as well know the truth of it." He stepped outside the door to look around. Satisfied that no one was nearby, he squatted at the doorway, looking at me. "The junk yard is an ideal place to stash bodies. The boss has done business with the Mafia before, lets them use this place when they need to. We first disable you, probably with chloroform, untie your hands, and put your body inside one of the cars way out in the back section. We got a crusher back there and—and—"

I sat stunned, unable to swallow past a dry throat, ignoring the perspiration oozing from my body. I could wake up in the middle of the crushing. Why didn't Jordan just shoot me?

"Surely there would be…ah…smells to alert authorities."

"Uh, uh. In this weather, bodies dry up fast." He left before he could say another word.

Well, that wasn't encouraging? If I told them where the money was, I would still be dead. If I didn't tell, eventually Dugan and Fern would get the money from the chandelier and possibly could figure out what to do with it. But so far, I'd not been able to offer any proof that the corporation was involved. Would Fern and Dugan go to the FBI? Jordan said he suspected George of working for them, which I found just plain idiotic.

Sleeping was out of the question, but I dozed off and on, with ugly dreams intruding until I forced myself to stay awake. I could tell the next morning turned cloudy and was thankful. The entire day passed. I needed to walk and unstiffen my legs but I grew weaker with no water or food. If only I could move around, walk and get some of the soreness worked out of my body, but I didn't have the energy to stir. At first my hands hurt where the rope burned in, but now they just stayed numb at the end of my arms. When I closed my eyes, I saw myself waking up inside a locked car and the ones above me gradually crunching down. Still no one came to the door.

Chapter 22

As night descended, I leaned back against the now cold metal wall, trying to stay awake. The dreams were much worse than what I imagined with my eyes open. In the front of the lot I heard the big dog barking. He'd finally stopped coming by and sniffing at the door since I hadn't had any food to give him.

At the sound of someone messing with the lock, I was surprised. I hadn't heard anyone approach. My heart skipped a few beats when I realized the person out there didn't have a key and then heard the distinct snap of bolt cutters. I got to my feet and staggered forward.

"Edwina! Are you in there?"

Oh, my god, it was Fern. "Yes, here I am. But be careful, there's a dog—"

"He's okay, won't bother us for a while," she answered just as the lock fell to the ground and Fern and Dugan pushed through the door, as if each wanted to be the first inside.

At first they looked stunned. I must have been quite a sight, not my finest moment. They both ran across the room and hugged me or I would have fallen.

"How did you find me?" I almost blurted out, "What took you so long?" But that wouldn't have been very gracious under the circumstances.

"We'll tell you all about it when we get you out of here." Dugan's voice broke when he flashed the light around at my prison.

Fern gasped and I felt tears stream down her cheeks when she laid her head against mine.

Dugan bent to cut the ropes on my wrists, and I tried not to cry out at the pain. I had to move my arms slowly to my side. Otherwise, I felt they might break off at the shoulders.

Between them, they almost had to drag me out of the building, my legs no longer worked.

"Let me stand and breathe fresh air for a moment, and I think I can walk if you go slow. Can we do that? Or are we in danger?"

"We got a few extra minutes so go ahead," Dugan said. He reached and picked me up in his arms as if I'd been weightless. "Hold on and we'll get you in the car." He walked behind Fern who led the way to the front gate. I leaned my weary head against his chest for a moment, to enjoy the heady sensation of freedom. I expected to get a rush from the dog attacking but we were unhindered.

"You didn't kill the poor dog, did you?" I asked.

Fern actually giggled. "No, 'course not. He turned out to be a big help actually. Dugan just opened the office door, threw a piece of meat inside, and shut the door behind him. Luckily, they didn't lock the office. It would have taken him too long to use his handy dandy lock pickers."

Dugan set me gently on the back seat where I could stretch out. Fern scooted in beside me and sat close to make sure I didn't fall forward. The car gave a loud belch and then lurched ahead. He looked embarrassed for a moment when he turned to peer at Fern and me in the back seat.

I grinned and motioned him to get on with it. "I don't want to be here a second longer."

Fern offered another drink from the thermos she'd brought.

"How did you know I'd be thirsty?" I asked and leaned back against her after I'd taken my fill of water. I'd never cared for water but it tasted like the finest champagne.

"We'll get you home, cleaned up, and fill you with good food."

I sighed. "Oh boy, do I ever want to go home."

"You're not going home, Edwina dear. You're coming to my house at least until we get you beefed up again."

Just what I needed to get beefed up, but my pajamas *were* hanging on me, I'd just noticed.

"And lordy, lordy, what a smell." Fern held her nose and pointed to the offending PJs.

I would go to my grave before I told her or anyone of the disgusting, demeaning necessities I endured. They tried to break me but it just outraged me.

"I'd really rather go home," I protested.

"I don't think you can take care of yourself right now," Dugan said. "When Fern called to tell me that your door was open, I got a locksmith right over, and we changed every lock, so you can probably stay at home after Fern checks you out. Do you think we should take you to the hospital? Did they hurt you?" His voice sounded scratchy with concern.

"No, not the hospital. I'm okay. They didn't harm me. I just got some cuts and bruises trying to get out a Fern window."

She poked me with her elbow but not hard and gave me another swig from the thermos.

The porch light was on when Dugan pulled up in front of Fern's house and honked. Joe came slamming out to open the back car door. Between Dugan and Joe, they practically lifted me by my elbows and walked me up the steps and inside. Fern immediately shut off the front porch light. The thick drapes were all pulled in the front room and they sat me gently down on the couch.

I touched my pajama top. "Wait, I don't want to get your furniture nasty."

Fern reached out to hold my hands and gently rubbed the burn damage to my wrists.

Joe stood in the middle of the room, hands on hips, looking like steam might come out of his ears any time. "Where the hell have you been?" He turned to glare at Fern. "You said you were going to get Edwina, but why didn't you wait for me? When you said she'd been missing three days, I wanted to go to the cops but both of you said no. I shouldn't have listened to you two nuts, she looks like shit, for chrissake."

Fern walked up and touched his cheek. I feared he might bite her. "Sugar, there wasn't time to let you know. I called and you were on a fire, and we had to act fast. I'll tell you all about it later, got to take care of her now."

He looked a trifle mollified, but I noticed Dugan stayed as far away from Joe as he could manage and still keep his dignity.

"I'll run her a warm bath and get one of Joe's T-shirts and his pajama bottoms. You can roll up the legs. Then we will bring her back here and give her something to eat and we'll all talk." Fern said that all in one long breath.

Sounded perfect to me. But really all I wanted to do was close my eyes and sleep on something soft and clean. To put sleep before eating and bathing amazed me, but I had only dozed in cat naps at the junk yard, fearful someone would come in the night and kill me. When they did that, I wanted to know.

After Fern had helped me into the bath tub filled with lovely warm water, she made sure I was awake, pulled the glass shower door closed, and sat on the john while I bathed. It didn't take long, and then I stood, wobbly, and holding on to the shower gizmo.

She immediately opened the shower door and wrapped a huge towel around me and a smaller one around my head to sop up my wet hair. She helped me into Joe's clothes and, even though I just wanted to collapse in bed and sleep, I knew we had questions and answers to listen to.

Chapter 23

She maneuvered me into the kitchen where Dugan and Joe already sat drinking coffee. Joe had made a rich chicken broth and I drank it from a big cup. My hands were not steady enough to lift a spoon. I kept flexing my still-numb fingers, although that was painful, but I couldn't help but notice that my hands had turned almost white. I feared losing all feeling in them permanently.

"First, tell me how you knew where I was," I said, stalling for time. I dreaded reliving my ordeal and put it off as long as I could.

Both Dugan and Fern started talking at once and then Dugan grinned and sat back and let Fern have the floor. She didn't hesitate.

"I called all one morning and you didn't answer the phone. Then I called Levine's office and he hadn't seen you since you took the job with Mr. Moody."

Dugan frowned. "About those so called jobs—"

Fern waved him to silence. "Later you can fuss at her. Anyways, I called Dugan and we went to pay a visit to Moody who wasn't home. When we went into the backyard and saw the pile of car parts that he'd accumulated, we had the aha! moment. The junkyard. We figured Moody must be the same man who worked there."

Dugan took up the story. "Fern hid in the car. She thought someone inside would recognize her since you two had been there before." Another frown from Dugan telling me he didn't think that was the brightest thing we'd ever done. "I introduced myself and the man in the office told me his name was Moody." Dugan grinned at his audience of three. "It's a PI trick to get a person's name," he said modestly. "Anyway, I mentioned some part and when he looked out the window at Bruce, that's the name of my car," he said before we could ask, "I guess he wasn't impressed so he waved me into the junk yard and proceeded to ignore me after a warning to keep away from the back of the junk yard as it was dangerous. Of course, I didn't pay attention to that as maybe I should have. They have a big dog, you know."

I smiled. "I know, I fed him my sandwiches until they stopped giving me anything."

"Lucky for your generosity. I noticed the big ugly fellow on the back lot, sitting by a door to a metal shed. He didn't budge when I walked a little closer. Knowing you, I figured that's where they were holding you."

"I don't think they usually let the dog loose during the day. I noticed he was chained when we went there."

"Fern and I figured they wouldn't have a night watchman with the dog running around. The less people involved the less danger and Moody couldn't work day and night."

"There's a law against kidnapping in case you didn't know. I wondered why you didn't call in the forces to come rescue me instead of taking the chance of doing it yourself. And don't we have to report something to someone?"

"We couldn't be sure you were there, Edwina." Dugan raked a hand through his hair. "Besides, if we had called in the FBI, for example, it might have come up about the cash, and I wasn't ready to let that go yet until we unraveled the mystery of why George took it. So we just proceeded on our own."

I absorbed that and nodded in agreement.

"Now it's your turn, Edwina, if it isn't too painful." Joe patted my shoulder gently. I could see why he had attracted Fern.

I took a sip of coffee, luxuriating in the taste. To tell the truth, in my captivity I missed the coffee I normally drank all day long more than a lot of things.

"I awoke in the middle of the night when Moody broke into my bedroom. I knew it was Moody by the odor of stale beer and cigarettes. He shined a flashlight into my eyes and then touched his fingers to my neck. The next thing I knew, I was blindfolded, gagged and trussed up like a turkey for Thanksgiving."

Dugan interrupted. "Damn, I'm sorry I didn't get on the locksmith earlier, Edwina." He looked so guilty.

"Probably wouldn't have mattered. You showed me how someone could cut a hole in the sliding glass door in the front and open it. The alarm system wasn't working either. Remember, I cut if off after George died, too expensive."

Everyone just shook their heads.

"To get on with it, I woke up in the shed, alone. Moody must have had help carrying me out to the car and into the shed. He's a big strong ox of a man, but I'm not tiny. It must have been Jordan or Carroll from the corporation. They didn't seem to trust anyone but Moody." No one spoke, waiting for my story. "They tied my hands in front, thankfully, and I managed to get the nasty gag out of my mouth and then the blindfold off. Moody came in finally, in the afternoon, bringing me a sandwich and a small canteen. I feared eating or drinking anything. It could have been poisoned or at least drugged. But he assured me that wasn't the case, that I was supposed to talk to someone. He let me know it didn't matter about the blindfold, and I knew then they weren't going to let me go. "

"Did you know where you were?" Fern asked.

"Right away. I smelled stale gasoline and oil and when Moody came in the shed the light from the doorway showed me stacks of car parts in the rear."

"You'll make a detective yet," Dugan commented, winking at me.

"And?" Fern couldn't sit still, she was so eager to hear my story, but she did calm down enough to pour me another cup of coffee.

I told them about trying to look out the window and how I shoved the pieces of sandwich under the door when I heard the dog snuffing around. "I was sure they wouldn't poison me, they had questions to ask. In retrospect I should have kept the stale old thing, they didn't feed or water me for the next two days."

"Geeze, what creeps," Fern said.

"My suspicions proved true when Jordan came inside. He had a gun with a long thing on the end that must have been a silencer, as if the coward was afraid of me." I related what he said and their threat to squash me like a bug inside the car crusher.

All three of them sucked in a deep breath and the look on their faces told me a lot about my friends.

"We could have been an hour or a day too late." Fern's forehead puckered into that charming Basset Hound look.

"So your instincts were right. George's employers are behind it all," Joe said, patting Fern's shoulder.

"It may just be Jordan and Carroll. They're playing it close to the vest, and I can't see them letting too many people in on the scheme. They held back money from the

Mafia, thinking no one would care about a measly couple of hundred thousand, but I guess those wise guys don't want it known that someone could steal from them. By then, George had put two and two together, got inside the safe, and brought the money home for safekeeping."

"Oh, I meant to tell you, some of the money was marked with chips. Which makes me suspect George was working with the FBI. With his help, they could get the goods on the corporation money laundering and the Mafia's involvement" Dugan interjected.

"Jordan must have been frantic," Joe said.

"For sure. They'd searched the house and didn't find a trace of money. But they must have been certain George took it. Somehow I thought time was of the essence and if I didn't come up with answers they would get rid of me and search the house again. Moody was going to be dead along with me, he knew too much by then."

Silence surrounded us while everyone absorbed it all.

Finally, I spoke. "How did you find out the money was marked?" I asked Dugan.

"Got a friend in FBI. He wouldn't tell me anything about the case of course, but he did check out some of the bills and told me about the chips in some of them. I knew they had to be FBI chips. Who else would have needed to do that? Jordan and Carroll had planned to keep the money at first. They had no reason to chip it."

"Since George had written down the numbers that

led us to the junk yard and brought home the money, we have to assume he was working for the FBI. I knew he would never jeopardize his retirement, no matter how the gambling got to him."

"That's probably why the bureau could trust him. Maybe George wanted to give up his habit and didn't know how to do it."

I sure hoped that was the case.

Chapter 24

Fern led me upstairs to a bedroom where I collapsed on clean sheets and a soft mattress. I slept like I'd never slept before, not waking up until she shook my shoulder lightly.

"Okay, sleepy head, it's been almost ten hours. You need to go to the bathroom, get dressed, and then have some oatmeal and coffee."

Sounded beyond wonderful to me. I used a hand to pull my covers back and realized with happy relief that the pain and numbness had disappeared.

"Joe had a firehouse call, but Dugan will be here later and wants to go over things with you. By now, Moody will be at the junk yard, and they'll know you're gone."

I came downstairs, still clothed in Joe's shirt and PJ pants. "I've got to go home sooner or later, Fern. I need clothes if nothing else." I managed a giggle. "I feel lost without my purse."

She reached to take my hands. "How are you doing with these? I noticed you could brush your teeth and comb your hair."

I felt a surge of joy to know my hands weren't permanently damaged. "Fine, a few twinges now and again, but okay."

"I don't think it's safe for you to go home yet. Remember Moody and Jordan are still out there, knowing you're a threat."

I ate the oatmeal and drank several cups of coffee before Joe came back from the fire.

"Where's T Rex by the way?" I didn't feel my anxiety for the big pit bull as I normally would have on visiting them.

Joe just came in the door and must have heard us. He laughed. "We took him to a neighbor for now. As you know, he doesn't care for visitors and with both you and Dugan here, we thought—"

I raised my hand and smiled. "Never mind the explanation, I'm relieved. I'm sure he's a swell companion and maybe one day you'll teach him that strangers can be good people."

Fern shook her head at her husband. "Yeah, I wanted Joe to take him to obedience school. And for sure we need to get him neutered, but so far Joe's nixed both things."

"I think he'll mellow in time on his own. I don't want to change his personality too much. I like him like he is."

"You're right, changing his personality would be terrible," Fern said, half laughing, half serious.

I refrained from joining the ongoing family argument.

Joe went to bed while Fern and I watched a little TV. It wasn't long before Dugan knocked and came in. Fern made us all a late lunch and Joe came down stairs, rubbing his eyes.

I laid my sliced turkey sandwich down on the plate and regarded the three of them sitting around the kitchen table. "You guys have been beyond swell, but I want to go home."

Fern and Joe turned to Dugan to answer.

"Look at it this way, Edwina. Jordan will have someone watching your place twenty-four/seven, and Moody will try to track you down. We have to think of something that will wrap this all up in a tidy bundle. But so far it's a blank for me."

"It hinges on the money," Joe put in. "Until you guys figure out when to hand it over to the FBI, nothing's going anywhere."

A zinger of an idea rushed through my mind, and I had all I could do not to blurt it out. But it could only involve me and Joe, if it had any chance of working right. Then I might be rid of the whole predicament at once.

The next morning, I waited for Fern to go to her dentist appointment and, before I could lose my courage, called for a taxi to Joe's firehouse. I looked in the mirror and straightened one of Fern's redheaded wigs on my head, tucking in my hair. I looked totally different. When we reached the firehouse I asked the taxi to wait for me.

Some of the guys were busy doing things with hoses while the majority sat around a huge table drinking coffee. When I entered, all the men jumped to their feet, their eyes questioning.

I spied Joe at once. "'Morning, guys. I need to speak with Joe a minute if that's okay."

They all nodded and sat back down while Joe, staring at me as if I'd developed two heads and a tail, and came forward and motioned for us to go outside.

"What's up?" he asked. Mr. Cool, he recognized me, but didn't ask about the wig.

Yesterday I was so sure of myself but looking into Joe's dark eyes, I wondered what I was thinking. But I had to blunder on. It was the only solution that had come to me.

"I have a big favor to ask, Joe. Can you introduce me to your Mafia Don or at least point him out to me?"

He looked shaken for a minute before he regained his composure. Living with Fern on a day-to-day basis, I felt sure nothing could rock him for long.

"In the first place, he's not *my* Mafia Don. In the second, third and fourth, no way."

"But it's important." I took hold of his arm and shook him a little but there was no give. There, he was solid. "The money doesn't belong to the FBI. It's wrongfully or rightfully, depending how you look at it, the Mafia's. Jordan and Carroll stole it from them and then George stole it again. It's very complicated as you can see, but it boils down to the Mafia at the bottom."

"Maybe," Joe said carefully. "But what's that got to do with you meeting up with the Don?"

"Fern must have told you about the bookie harassing me for George's debts. I presumed he was part of the Mafia. In fact, the car he drove made me think he could be very high in that organization."

"What do you know about the car he drove?"

"I recognized the sound as the same vehicle my neighbor down the street used to drive when he turned around at the cul-de-sac. I thought it sounded like a Porsche and when I peeked out the gate, I saw a silver car."

Joe looked pensive, like he was putting it all together. "It could be Bella's, although I can't see him doing leg work. George must have owed them a bundle."

"Bella? Funny name for a Mafia Don."

"His last name. No one knows his first name."

"Oh. Well, getting on with it, I can wait for his next visit I suppose, but it might take a while. In the meantime I'm a marked person, aren't I?"

Joe managed a grin at my slang. "I'll do what I can, kiddo, but I don't like being obligated to anyone like that."

"It seems to me he will just be returning a favor. You guys saved his house, after all."

"Yes, well there's that. I'll get in touch."

"Thanks. I don't know what I'd do without you and Fern."

"She gets under your skin, doesn't she?" Joe laughed at my expression and turned to go inside.

இஅஇஅ

That afternoon, when Fern and Joe sat at the kitchen table with me, I decided it was time to go home.

"I need to go home," I echoed my thoughts with as much composure as I could dredge up. They had been so kind and giving.

To my amazement, both Fern and Joe nodded. "I think it will be okay now," Fern said. "Dugan had new locks installed on all your doors and windows, and he ordered a reinstallation of your burglar alarm."

"That was thoughtful. I'm hoping one day soon I'll be able to pay him for his time."

"Not to worry. He's anything but impatient, and I believe he cares for you beyond a client relationship."

I felt a warm blush cover my cheeks. "Not a good idea."

"I only meant that he considers you a friend," Fern protested.

"I can take you home and look around the place before you go in," Joe offered.

Knowing he'd just got off work for the night, I shook my head. "I'll be fine."

He stood up to leave for his bedroom and I reached out to hug him. "You guys are the best. I can never repay you for what you have done for me."

He hugged back and then pushed me gently away, looking embarrassed. "You're a good friend. Anything we can do…"

Fern and I went upstairs to the guest bedroom while Joe stayed behind for another cup of coffee before lying down. We finished packing what little I'd brought and Fern gave me a big hug.

"Take care, girlfriend. Just call if you need to talk or anything. I'll be over in a few days after you get settled."

"You're the best. No one could ask for a better friend. You're the sister I never had."

Fern looked uncomfortable. We seldom expressed our mutual feelings. Finally, she managed, "I know. I feel the same, in spite of having four sisters, you are number one." She moved away to close a suitcase. "I think Joe called a taxi."

I picked up one suitcase and she got the other. Even though the case wasn't heavy, it felt like a hurtful strain on my arm. I refrained from rubbing it, knowing Fern would grab the suitcase from me.

Downstairs, she opened the door and, sure enough, a taxi waited. She put a suitcase on the back seat along with mine and I kissed her cheek and waved goodbye, getting into the cab.

When he pulled up into my driveway, I heaved a sigh

of relief to see the place again. As much as I had never cared for the ostentatious look of it, for now at least, it was home.

Chapter 25

I used the new set of keys Dugan had given me and, upon entering, stopped a moment to check if I had any gut feelings of someone coming inside again. To my relief, I felt an empty house.

"George," I said out loud and the words echoed in the high ceiling. "I didn't ask for all of this, why couldn't we have talked about it? Why didn't you stay a professor?"

Since his death, I had slowly begun to realize that he was so sure he knew what I wanted and needed but he never liked his work.

I took a suitcase upstairs into the bedroom and came down for the other one. The house was cold as a tomb and I didn't know how long I'd have to stay here alone. The good recollections I could absorb gratefully, but the bad ones of late…

Later, I went into the bright, shiny kitchen and made

a half-hearted omelet. George usually did the cooking. He said he enjoyed it after a day's work. I picked up the slack on weekends with potato salad and marinated steaks for George to grill. The house felt as if it closed in around me, wrapping me with memories that had become suffocating. After drinking two cups of black coffee and eating part of breakfast, I went into the dining room and lowered the chandelier. I took out several stacks of money and let it up again. I watched as the glass tinkled, a bit more cheerfully than I felt.

Fern and Dugan called every day to check on me, probably sensing that I wanted some alone time. Not that I hadn't had my fill of it during my kidnapping. I wondered that the bank hadn't called, since there were no messages on the land line.

Three days after I returned home, I stood on my back terrace when I heard the definite purring of a car coming toward the cul-de-sac. I sat on a wicker chair and waited. I couldn't decide if fear or curiosity held me in thrall but my heart beat faster as the big silver car turned into my driveway and stopped in front of the door.

I recognized the man getting out as Bent Nose but he had changed drastically in every way but his features. He wore a suit that I recognized as probably costing many hundreds of dollars with a striped white and blue shirt and a tie. When he came closer, I noticed the color of his shirt matched his blue eyes. How odd. I had stereotyped him as Italian, of course with dark eyes, but, in fact, when he came to the house before I'd never actually been able to look him in the face.

"Mrs. Hartley?" He moved cautiously up the steps as if not wishing to alarm me. In spite of his expensive clothing, he still looked like an ex-boxer or wrestler.

"Yes? You are Mr. Bella?" I didn't know if I was allowed to actually use his name but I persevered.

He nodded and I gestured for him to be seated on a nearby chair. We didn't shake hands, which was fine with me.

Clearing his throat, he said, "You wanted to speak with me?"

The voice was still gravelly. I'd assumed that was a put on to scare me but, apparently, it was real.

As if he noticed my surprise when he spoke, he pointed to his throat. "Cancer. It's okay now. Just took away my tenor voice."

I smiled at his attempt of humor. "I imagine that was a great loss."

He smiled too, and his features arranged themselves almost pleasantly.

"Please come inside. I am going to tell you a strange story, and I hope you will believe me. I have no reason to lie to you."

Upon opening the door, Bella took out some kind of hand held gizmo. "May I?" he asked.

I must have looked puzzled.

He shrugged as if it wasn't important. "It's a bug catcher, to put it in layman's terms."

"You think I might have ah…bugged my home?"

"Oh, no, not you, per se. But someone might have."

I gestured for him to continue, and he turned the light on, sweeping his hand around the room and up to the ceiling. "I don't need to go upstairs," he said. "Sounds don't carry that far."

When he had finished, he put the instrument back in his jacket pocket and sat where I'd motioned for him to sit, near the dining room table.

I took a deep breath and began with George's gambling vice and, even though I felt traitorous, I went on to tell him about his cashing in our insurance policies and maybe losing his retirement when Jordan, the CEO of GG&W, accused him of embezzlement.

"George had many faults, as you can see by now, but he never would have stolen from the corporation and risked his retirement. He was looking forward to that."

Bella nodded, his hands folded over his stomach, waiting patiently for me to continue.

When I reached the part of George's death and how and why I believed it was murder, he frowned, his dark eyebrows crashing together. He looked like a Mafia Don then.

"We had nothing to do with that," he said vehemently.

"Oh, I never thought you had. Otherwise, you wouldn't have tried to collect the debt George owed you."

He looked chagrined. "I apologize if I frightened you. It's just that many people pull a disappearing act to try and get rid of their debt, and I wanted to make sure that wasn't happening here. I don't collect from widows—unless they are the ones gambling."

That gave me a surge of relief. I offered coffee or tea and to my surprise he asked if I had any herbal tea. Of course I did, and as soon as I'd microwaved us both cups, I brought it back out on a tray.

When I sat again, I told him about my kidnapping. "I don't suppose you had anything to do with that?" I tried to keep my tone light so as not to annoy him.

He did look pained when he said, "We don't operate like that."

"I didn't think so. Anyway, to get to why I wanted to speak to you…" I pushed the button and lowered the chandelier. I'd already hidden some of the stacks away, thinking I might need them for the FBI.

A flair of satisfaction hit me as I saw maybe for the first in a long time, the Don was flabbergasted. Finally he took out a pen from his pocket and reached inside the glass to retrieve a stack to set it on the table, scooting his chair closer, letting out a low whistle.

I admired his desire not to leave fingerprints but that came a little late. I waited.

His eyebrows lifted and his forehead wrinkled. "Who does all this belong to?"

"I suppose to you, even though it was acquired illegally. Who can prove that? This is money Jordan and Carroll skimmed from your organization when they laundered money for your organization. Since they are an accounting firm, they were able to hide it, and were careful not to take too much."

He pounded his fist on the table. "Madam, one dollar is too much to steal from us. We cannot allow it. Bad for business if it gets out that someone was able to appropriate funds from our—organization. Do you suppose anyone else in GG and W was involved?"

"I don't know for sure, but I don't think so. Jordan and Carroll didn't seem to trust anyone."

"How did the money come to you?"

I realized he knew George must have brought it home, and he waited for me to confirm this. "My husband hid it away. I think he felt threatened by Jordan, and thought this would keep him safe. Obviously…"

He cleared his throat. "We have done business with this Jordan person. You are certain he is the one who skimmed us?"

"I'm sure of it. Carroll, his second in command, might be involved, but Jordan is the brains behind it all. George had it on his computer in a hidden file." I didn't want to say what else was in that file. I figured it was important for Bella not to feel threatened in any way if I wanted his help.

"So you are saying this money essentially belongs to us?" He looked at the piles in the bottom of the chandelier.

I shrugged. "Who else? Jordan took it from you, and George relieved it from him. It's not that I condone illicit money laundering, if that is the case here, but you can see my problem. The money has to go somewhere."

"You could have quietly kept it for yourself." His eyes were piercing, his tone gentle. He leaned back in his chair and rubbed his forehead with his hand, waiting for my answer.

"I'm not saying it never occurred to me," I admitted. "But truth be told, while I'm not a goody-goody, and it's no reflection on you, I wasn't raised that way and neither was George. That's why it's so puzzling to me as to how he acquired the money."

"I can't imagine. But we are aware that the FBI is watching this accounting firm. We have a janitor inside who knows the phones in the executive offices are monitored."

"Are you threatened by the involvement of the FBI?"

He barked out a laugh. "Not really, as long as we stay informed. Are there ah...any strings attached to the money?

"No. But I have to warn you, George may have been involved in an ongoing FBI investigation of GG and W."

"It figures. Thank you for your honesty in telling me that. However, we can take care of ourselves with government officials."

I didn't want to know how that worked. "If I give you your money back, that won't bring justice for

George. The FBI may eventually drop their investigation. And even if they prove anything against the corporation heads, it would probably wind up a seven or eight year sentence. I have no court admissible proof they killed George, but I did find evidence of it."

He reached out to pat my hand, his fingers softer and warmer than mine. It brought a shiver down my spine to think this strong, powerful man laid his cards out on the table with no witnesses.

"Don't you worry," he said. "We'll take care of everything. I can't abide loose ends."

I pushed the stack of hundreds toward him.

He chuckled, the sound rasping deep in his throat. "You are a very brave woman. If I didn't have a family and was a few years younger..."

No way Jose. That was very gallant of him, since we must have been the same age. I smiled and accepted the compliment, as I watched while he tucked the money into the inside pocket of his suit jacket.

As soon as he left I needed to call Fern and Dugan to tell them what I'd done.

Chapter 26

Dugan was the first to arrive the next morning. He sputtered and carried on as if I were the most stubborn and irresponsible person he'd ever met. "You should have called me to witness this crazy exchange. What were you thinking, giving the Mafia all that money? What about the FBI? Eventually, they will have to know all about this caper."

When he finally ran down, I shifted in my chair. We were seated at the dining room table, under the chandelier and its unseemly decadence. I chuckled. "Caper?"

He flicked his hand to tell me I was being facetious. I knew it without him telling me. But that was too hard to pass up.

"Don't change the subject."

Just then Fern rang the doorbell, and I invited her into the dining room. She and Dugan greeted each other. Dugan was the first to speak.

"Go on, tell her what you were beginning to tell me."

When I related almost all of the conversation between me and the Don, silence reigned in the big room
reaching all the way up to the ceiling.

Suddenly Fern leaped up from her seat and ran over
to hug me. "Joe would say you got *cajones,* woman. I just
wish I could have been a fly on the wall."

Dugan frowned and I laughed, hugging her back.

"Were you scared?" Fern wanted to know.

"A little," I admitted.

"How'd you manage to get a Don to come here anyway?" Dugan demanded.

Fern and I avoided eye contact. No use involving
Joe. That would take too much explaining.

"You do know we have to go to the FBI soon,"
Dugan said.

"I held some money back." I went to the drawer and
pulled out a stack.

We talked for a while and, as they were leaving,
Dugan and I made an appointment for the next day to visit the FBI. I found a name, M. Nichols, on George's
computer that somehow connected to the agency so figured I'd ask for him.

ℰᴖℰᴖ

It took a while, and we waited patiently in the
cramped, dingy office. Couldn't the government afford
better or was this a kind of covert place? I was learning

new words by the day. I had put the stack of money in a bank zippered bag and held it nestled to my body, under my arm, hidden by my suit jacket. It didn't fit into my purse.

Finally we were ushered into Nichol's office. We all shook hands and I introduced Dugan and myself.

"How can I help you?" was his first question.

I took a deep breath and told him most of my story. Except the part about *all* the money and the Mafia. When I'd finished, he sat studying me thoughtfully, his gray eyes reminding me of a storm at sea.

Dugan and I waited. I could tell he was a little disturbed by the way his foot lightly tapped under his chair, but he hid it well.

I maneuvered the bag from my jacket, emptying it on his desk. His eyes flared and, for a moment, I thought he might pull out a gun, but he settled back and waited.

"Mrs. Hartley's deceased husband George ah…lifted this from GG and W, the accounting firm she told you about. I believe it has been chipped or marked in some way."

He turned to look at me. I knew what he asked. Had I informed the Mafia about this possibility? Unfortunately, it must have slipped my mind.

The agent gingerly picked up a bundle. He no doubt knew it had been handled and there would be no tell-tale fingerprints. He called on his speaker phone and when a man came to the door, Nichols handed him a package.

"Check it," he said briefly. The man left with the money.

"Did your husband own a computer?"

Odd question. I thought a moment. "Yes, of course. He used one at the office and had one at home."

He folded his fingers together, elbows on the desk. "We may need to take a look at that down the line."

"Certainly." If they could get into the computer and find out about the Mafia, there wasn't anything I could do about that. They would eventually subpoena the computers at the accounting firm anyway.

We waited in silence and, when the man came back with the money, he nodded, set it on the desk, and left.

"Well, well," Nichols said. "I can tell you that the money was indeed chipped and looks as if our agency did it. How astute of you to deduce that, Mr. Dugan."

I grinned as Dugan straightened his shoulders and acknowledged the compliment with a brief nod. *Mr. Cool.*

Nichols stood and held out his hand to shake ours. "If that is all, we appreciate your integrity in bringing this to our attention. I cannot go into details at this time, but I assure you we are exploring the situation, and it will be resolved in the near future. Meanwhile, should anything else come up pertaining to this matter, please do not hesitate to let me know."

He pushed a buzzer and the outside man came to escort us out. He asked us to wait while he issued a receipt for the money I left behind.

On the way home, Dugan was quiet. He finally asked

me, "Edwina, do you feel any guilt or anxiety about giving the Mafia back a portion of their money and holding out some for the FBI?"

Was he thinking I'd double-crossed both of them? I hoped not. I would be devastated to lose Dugan's respect. "No, I feel as if that was the only way to handle it and get out with my own skin intact. The agency will eventually discover the Mafia's part in this, but the mob can take care of their own. It's an even match."

We were getting close to home, and I knew he had more questions.

"So how does this sit with you, no revenge for George's death?"

"I wasn't exactly seeking revenge, Dugan. I wanted justice. We'll just have to wait and see. But I want to thank you for all your help and standing by me. I'll soon be able to settle up with you."

He reached over to touch my shoulder. "Never mind, sweetheart. You done good, and if you can't pay me a dime, I'm satisfied. I just wish you didn't work for Levine."

I smiled, not answering. It had been interesting working for the ogre, and I might take on a few more cases, who knew?

Chapter 27

As the days passed, Fern and I went about packing up the belongings in the house that I wanted to keep. When I finished, Joe came and took the lot to a nearby storage unit.

On an unforgettable Saturday morning, Fern came ringing the doorbell in that irritatingly insistent way she had. I opened the door.

"Edwina, you gotta see this!" She waved a newspaper in front of my face, startling me. I no longer subscribed to the paper, thinking it an unnecessary expense.

She pulled me to the couch and, while we sat, she spread the paper out on our laps. I fumbled for my reading glasses in the pocket of my sweater while she fidgeted with impatience.

"For gosh sakes, forget the glasses. I'll read it for you."

"Never mind. Here they are, and calm down before you have a stroke."

I looked down at a brief article on the back page.

The article read: *A body was recently recovered from the East River. Identified as Jonathan Jordan, there was no indication of foul play and the coroner ruled it a suicide.*

We looked at each other, speechless. The Don said they would take care of things. Had they? Or had Jordan grown despondent with the upcoming investigation? I felt not even a twinge of pity for the man. I knew in my heart of hearts that he'd caused poor George's death.

Nichols called a week later, telling me that the investigation with GG&W had been resolved. As usual, he was tight-lipped with his information.

"Does that mean the accounting firm will close?"

"Not at all. Seems as if only the two corporate heads were presumed guilty of fraud and money laundering. Carroll and Jordan. If you've kept up with the news, unfortunately Mr. Jordan will be unavailable for questioning. By the way, we have cleared up the situation about any embezzling charges against your husband with the firm."

Lordy, lordy, that would mean George's retirement would be there.

"Also," he added as if with afterthought, "there will be an award for you and your husband posthumously, for helping with the criminal indictment."

I took a deep breath, enough to thank him and hung up, sitting down heavily in the nearest chair.

I might be able to afford the house now, but it was no longer important to me. I would call Junior, tell him only a small portion of what had happened and that his father was a hero. Then I might get in touch with Levine and work another case, just for fun. I'd get Fern to help this time, knowing how much she would enjoy an adventure. I enjoyed detecting so much I might even ask Dugan if I could work part time in his office.

"I'll be leaving here soon, George," I said looking up at the chandelier. "But I'll take the memories along with, me, and you can be sure the angels are sleeping well now."

About the Author

Born in Phoenix, Arizona, Pinkie Paranya traveled all over the US, Alaska, and most of Mexico with her late husband. Ever since she can remember, writing has been her passion. After completing her fifteenth novel, trying to discover the genre she loved most, she still hasn't decided.

Paranya enjoys romances with their intrigue and uplifting happy endings, but she has also published two paranormal psychological suspenses, a cozy mystery, and an Early American Alaskan trilogy. To date, she has fifteen published novels.